The Hour of Atonement

By

Kasey Marlatt

Case ID: **1-15121087271**

LCCN: **2026907490**

ISBN: **978-1-971232-65-2**

Website: https://kaseymarlatt.com

First Edition

ACKNOWLEDGEMENT

To my wife, Traci, you are my rock, my everything. I could not have accomplished any of this without your unwavering love and support.

Pawpaw, you inspired me to always give my best effort and to always believe in myself. We all miss you down here. See you when I get there.

My friend Bill Stubblefield, thank you for all of your encouragement and for all of the good times. Your constant support was essential to keeping me motivated to finish writing this book.

TABLE OF CONTENTS

PREFACE

Out of the small smoke-filled caverns of small-town bars and the loneliness of small towns across America, there exists a segment of mankind that are souls of times gone by. Dependent on no one and beholden to no one, they are often loners who forge their own path through life. Whether it be due to socio-economic status, skin color, or religion, many of these somewhat reclusive loners are viewed as odd and unnatural and are forced to live outside the social circles of the "proper" citizens. These outcasts often form lifelong bonds of friendship amongst each other that couldn't be broken by any device of mankind or mortal treachery, but more often than not, last until the last heartbeat, until the last breath, or until reckoning and revenge have had their day. When the times come to pass that bring you to a place so desolate that you can't determine whether it would be better to wake up tomorrow or slip away into the sands of time during the hours of darkness before dawn, It is these lifelong friendships that often drag people along and motivate them to get up and go out for one more day in the muck and mire of a mortal existence.

CHAPTER 1

The bright light of the morning sun blazed through the window like an emotionless being hunting some doomed prey. The prior evening's festivities still pounded inside Jim's head. Jim sat up and forced himself to the edge of the bed. He felt lost, as if he had woken up in a changed world. He felt uneasy and confused. He told himself it was just the hangover. He slowly rose to his feet, hanging on to the bedpost for balance. He swayed and limped his way to the bathroom across the brutal beam of window light. He made his way to the bathroom and showered, shaved, and stood in front of the mirror. He looked out of the bathroom into the cavern of darkness from whence he came. The beam of light made the rest of the bedroom seem like a dark cave. He glanced back at the bathroom mirror, then at the small calendar that stayed stuck to the bottom right corner. It was September 17th, 4 years since he had moved into this house, and 4 years since he lost half of his small amount of wealth to a now ex-wife. He referred to this day as his liberation from darkness, and his friends usually needled him about it every year. But this year, it was different. Jim was determined not to let the past eat at him on this day. He wanted a day filled with thoughts provoked by a new day, unaffected by past wounds. Despite his best efforts, he knew that it was an impossible task.

After getting dressed, Jim slowly made his way down the hall, past the two other empty bedrooms, and into the living room. He crossed the living room to the couch and sat down. He loved the forest green walls of his living room, even though most people told him it looked like a dungeon. He grabbed the TV remote, powered on his TV, and changed the channel to reruns of King of the Hill. Jim enjoyed uplifting programming on dark days such as this.

September 17, 2010

"Jim, they want all the property and all the investments, for you to assume the mortgage, and for you to transfer the title of your truck and camping trailer, which you own free and clear." The short bald lawyer told him.

"Mike, no way. No goddamn way. I'll sit my ass in jail for whatever contempt I get before I agree to that," Jim retorted.

"I know that, Jim; that's what I told them, but in a nicer, legal way," Mike Prescott, Jim's attorney, said.

"She wants the house, but if we can't agree, the judge has said that we will have to sell it, right?" Jim asked

"That's correct," Mike responded while looking inquisitively at Jim.

"Here's what you tell them: We will have to sell the house and split the proceeds. If she wants it, she will have to buy it. I don't want her money or her retirement. She keeps the checking account and her retirement; I keep the mutual funds because the money I made off of them went to her college expenses. I think it's fair that I keep the mutual funds. Tell them that and see what they say."

Mike made no response; he gathered his papers and left the room. Jim's wife, Christine, was in the next room with her attorney. Christine had just graduated from college when she was caught sleeping with Jim's boss. It had been going on for the entire marriage. Jim was devastated when he found out. It took only 3 weeks to get to this point in the divorce process. Jim refused to be in the same room with Christine or her attorney, which is why they were conducting somewhat unconventional negotiations. Jim could hear Mike relaying his message. He could also hear Christine say in a crying voice, "I just want the house, no matter what, I want the house." That was the unexpected bargaining chip that Jim needed.

After fifteen minutes of cold suspense, Mike returned.

"She absolutely wants the house," Mike said.

"I heard," Jim responded.

"When I told her that we were ready to sell the house and split the money, she backtracked. She will agree to your terms on the money, on the condition that she can assume the mortgage on the house, removing your name and releasing you from it. She just wanted the 18 grand ya'll had in the checking account. Her attorney told her that the judge would make them sell it, and he recommended making this counteroffer. She still says she doesn't want the divorce." Mike explained.

"People in hell want ice water." Jim retorted.

"Tell her I will agree on one condition: she may not contact me directly on the phone for any reason. If she wishes to contact me, she has to do it in writing through her attorney. If it costs her money to contact me, she will leave me alone." Jim said.

"Ok," Mike replied as he left the room. It was over.

Now, four years later, he still felt the sense of finality that he felt that day. It was as if his life restarted at that moment. He had received more than fifty letters from her attorney, begging him to agree to a meeting. Jim refused each time. Word had gotten back to Jim through friends that Christine had blown the 18,000 she got on plastic surgery, vacations, and stupid business decisions. All she was left with was the house, and she was now near bankruptcy. Jim turned his thoughts to Hank Hill on the television. He began to laugh and felt the pain vacate his thoughts, and the day suddenly seemed a bit more bearable.

"Let me in, the sun is frying my brain!!" Someone yelled from the door. Jim recognized the voice of Travis Livingston, one of his few close friends.

"Why the hell did you knock? You should have just come on in," Jim said as he opened the door. "Well, I wouldn't want to disturb all the crazy ass demons running around in your brain on this day, it might make me forget what a lucky, good-looking son of a bitch I am. When you're good-looking your whole life, it's easy to take for granted," Travis explained with a big grin on his face.

"If horse shit was money, you would be retired in Jamaica" Jim retorted while laughing.

"So, what is on your agenda today, Mr. Doom and Gloom? You going to drink beer in the dark, or are you going to defile yourself in a manner which will allow a public viewing of the spectacle?" Travis prodded.

"I think I'm going to go by the office and check on things, and then get drunk," Jim explained with a half-smile on his face.

"Scratch the getting drunk and come with me to look at that place for sale south of town, I want an astute businessman's opinion," Travis said as he got up and headed to the kitchen.

Jim knew he was looking for coffee and said, "I haven't made any coffee yet. You talking about that place with the big barn and 40 acres?" Jim asked and stared at the ceiling while he waited for another smart ass reply from Travis.

"Yep, if I'm going to get it, I need to move fast. That doctor looked at it yesterday, but he didn't look inside the house." Travis explained.

"Why not?" Jim asked.

"Because I purposefully forgot to return the key to the realtor yesterday. Mainly, because I don't want that uppity asshole to buy it from underneath me." Travis explained while trying not to chuckle. "How nice of you." Jim retorted. After conceding failure on his caffeine-seeking venture, Travis meandered back into the living room and sat in the recliner.

"Come by here at two o'clock, and we will head down there." Jim proposed as he walked to the front door.

"You bringing the beer or me?" Travis inquired, smiling as he stood.

"You invited me, so I will expect a six-pack of Coors Light." Jim said as he opened the door, signaling Travis to leave him alone and let him get on with the day.

"OK, see you at two, with a case of bottles, major financial decisions can't be made on a mere six-pack." Travis proclaimed as he walked out the door. Jim watched him leave and laughed. It would be a good day today. Jim sat back down on the couch in time to observe the end of Hank Hill's propane exploits. As the tale of Hank, Dale, and Boomhauer came to an end, Jim gathered his wallet, cell phone, and truck keys. He pulled his boots on and put on his jacket, then headed towards the door.

Jim pulled up the stop sign and waited for Highway 31 to clear. The main highway through town was laid out like a long black snake winding through the wooded hills and cow pastures. A semi was slowly making its way from his left. It seemed to move slowly, as if it had no concept of time. If traffic allowed, Jim always stayed a few extra minutes at this stop sign, just to look at the large field across the highway and to look at the winding stair mountains in the distance. He brought himself back out of his scenery-driven trance and turned west toward town. Twenty minutes later, Jim pulled into one of his two convenience stores, the other of which lay in the next town over, 22 miles away. He got out of his truck and saw the place about half full, which was normal for this time of day. Jim never came into his office during the morning rush, because everybody wanted to stop and talk, and there were relatively few people he cared to converse with about the goings on of the world. He walked in the back door and immediately looked at the floors. He despised dirty floors.

"Stella, somebody needs to sweep!" he yelled. He had never quite mastered the art of subtlety. "Ok, we will get on it." Stella hollered from the other side of the store as she was straightening up the chip aisle. Jim walked out of the store area toward his office. Rashad, a cashier, emerged from behind the counter and followed Jim.

"What do you need, Rash?" Jim inquired without looking at Rashad.

"Can I get off early today? The clinic called, and they had a cancellation, and I can get my new glasses today." Rashad asked while being obviously nervous.

"Who is covering for you?" Jim responded, turning to him.

"Jamie said she could come in an hour early," Rashad explained.

"Good with me, call Jamie and tell her. I'm going with Travis this afternoon to look at some property he is trying to buy, so I will be out of here about 1:30," Jim explained and then walked away. Rashad hurried away, obviously excited to be able to leave early. Jim looked over the previous day's deposits, the fuel inventory, and the previous day's sales. He approved the schedule for the next week that Stella had prepared, then he signed the checks for the bills. With his office tasks for the day concluded, he called Travis.

"Hello, it's too early for you to be calling me to be in compliance with our prearranged schedule, so what's changed, Mr. Doom?" Travis asked in a chiding reference to Jim's demeanor.

"I'm done at the office; It's Stella's shift this afternoon. I'm free to look at your possible new abode, if you're free." Jim explained.

"Pick you up in twenty minutes," Travis said and then hung up.

CHAPTER 2

The wind blew a white plastic Walmart sack across the parking lot as Jim watched it. It reminded him of his honeymoon with Christine. It was so windy the first day of their honeymoon that trash and paper were blowing all over their hotel's parking lot. Even though he despised the woman, he still reflected fondly on the good times he had with her. They were madly in love at one point in time. They had driven all the way to New Orleans, with two weeks to do anything they wanted. Jim had just gotten a big promotion at the firm where he worked, and he was excited to be able to give his new wife the honeymoon she wanted. He had longed to hear some live music and to eat some good Cajun food. When they had gotten to the hotel, Christine changed clothes quickly, and they spent that entire afternoon walking around the city, talking about the future, kids, and how happy they were with each other. Now as he sat on the bench outside of his store, Jim wondered how someone could change to what Christine had become. Jim saw his old boss, Devon, from time to time. Devon was now a clerk at a Home Depot store, fired after he was caught sleeping with a client on several occasions. Devon's reputation was ruined, and he wasn't able to salvage his career. Jim considered it poetic justice, and it was that example of karma that kept Jim from punching Devon every time the two crossed paths. The bench in front of the store was one of Jim's favorite places; it always seemed to be in the shade, and it gave a perfect view of downtown Bellville. The sun always shone down into the parking lot beyond, illuminating the parking lot like fire shining down from above. Even on hot days such as this, Jim liked it out here. The heat reminded him that he was mortal, and the bench always kept him in touch with his humble beginnings. The gray ford of Travis's caught Jim's eye as it pulled into the parking lot. The ford pulled into the parking spot in directly in front of him. Jim could see the ray ban sunglasses, the same Purina feed ball cap, and the same look on Travis's face that made everybody who saw him think that he was fixing to crack the funniest joke of all time. Jim rose to his feet and began to walk toward the ford. Jim tried the door, it was locked. He looked up at Travis.

"I open that door on one condition. You don't say one word about that whore ex-wife of yours," Travis demanded.

"Deal," Jim responded.

Travis unlocked the door, and Jim climbed into the passenger seat. The inside was immaculate as always. The gray interior always looked as if it had been driven off the lot the previous day. Jim reclined his seat slightly and said, "Ok, what are you thinking this place is worth?" Jim asked Travis as he tried to get his seat adjusted to get comfortable.

"200 tops. I say that for two reasons. One, the place with 53 acres down the road sold for 225, and this place doesn't have as nice a barn as the other place. Two, I don't want to give more than 200 for it." Travis explained.

"I think that's fair money, I would take it if it was me selling." Jim agreed. The two pulled out of the parking lot and headed south out of town. 10 minutes later, they were pulling into the driveway of the house Travis wanted to buy. The living room window was open and a TV could be seen playing in the living room.

"That son of a bitch!" Travis cursed as he saw the TV. "I bet that fat curly-headed fuck is sitting in there watching TV." Travis continued as his frustration was almost comical to Jim.

"The hell with them, you can find another place." Jim tried to console Travis as Travis began to purse his lips and nod his head slowly, which was a sure sign of an impending eruption of anger.

"Fuck that!" Travis said as he opened his door and began to briskly walk toward the front door. Travis put his key in the lock, opened the door, and stepped inside.

Jim waited for what seemed like an eternity before he finally saw Travis standing at the front door with something in his hand. The mystery object revealed itself when Travis threw it into the driveway.

Travis had stolen the gentleman's remote and thrown it forty yards into the driveway. Travis walked at the same brisk pace back to the truck.

"I'm guessing the doc has made a recent real estate purchase," Jim said

"You goddamn right he did. For 180,000, paid fully in advance yesterday." Travis explained while resuming his slight head nod.

"He paid for it all yesterday. Nobody had looked at it, but you, and you told the realtor you were going to make an offer." Jim said while fighting off the urge to get good and pissed off himself.

"He didn't take one look at it before he bought it, he said. That's what happens when idiots have money." Travis concluded as he pulled out his cell phone. He dialed a number and pushed the speaker phone button. It rang four times when a woman answered the phone.

"Samuels Realty, Nicole speaking." The voice said. "Nicole, this is Travis Livingston. I want to make an offer of 265,000 for the house we spoke about yesterday." Travis said into the phone. Jim laughed when Travis gave the offer of 265,000, knowing Travis would ring this one for all it was worth, and then some. "Wow, umm hang on," Nicole responded. She could be heard talking to another person for a couple of minutes.

"Mr. Livingston, I am so sorry, but we received a higher offer yesterday and the house is in contract already," Nicole responded once she returned to the line.

"You're lying. I'm sitting in the driveway of the house now, watching that curly-headed smart ass watch TV. I just had a conversation with the doc just now and I know that he offered 180,000. You lied to me; therefore, I regret to inform you that you can go to hell." Travis explained and then hung up.

"There, I feel better now. Let's get drunk" Travis proposed as Jim raised a beer and toasted Travis. "Sounds like a plan," Jim responded as he took a big drink.

Travis and Jim had been driving around back roads for two hours when they decided to head back toward Jim's store.

"You know what we need, Trav? A vacation!" Jim proclaimed, as if he were sure that it would cure all of their problems.

"Yes, we do, except I don't want any big city, someplace in the country. A camping trip, maybe. Get out on the water, do some fishing, even though I'm not that damn good at it. Lefty would like to get away to," Travis replied cheerfully.

Lefty was Travis's best friend. The two men were closer than brothers. Lefty was a nickname for Edward Whitehorse. Jim didn't know exactly how he got the nickname, but Travis had always said that he thought it came from when he was a child learning to talk because left was his first word. Travis said that he would say "left, left, left" over and over when he was little. Jim had never asked Lefty about it, but always judged Travis's theory as plausible.

"Is Lefty still working for the Choctaws?" Jim asked Travis.

"Yeap. It's the damnedest thing. A Comanche working as a security guard for the Choctaws, and as a hunting guide for a bunch of Choctaw Indians on the side. I guess these civilized Indians around here need a real Indian to teach them how to hunt," Travis theorized as he laughed.

"I guess. I'm a sixteenth, and I couldn't tell you how my ancestors hunted or lived. Lefty could, though," Jim added.

"Yeap, he could. He is coming over tonight. Come over for supper, and we'll discuss vacationing like we are worthy enough to experience any form of relaxation," Travis suggested.

"I'll be there about 7:30," Jim responded.

They finally pulled into the store. Jim stumbled out of the truck and into the front door. He didn't care about trying to hide the fact that he enjoyed getting drunk every once in a while.

"Hey boss, got mail today. You will want to see it," Stella informed him as he entered the store. She was giddy and excited, which usually meant some good news came in the mail.

"Ok, I'll read it if I can make it to my office without falling," Jim retorted.

He walked down the hall and sat down at his desk. He could see a letter addressed to him from the city of Bellville. He opened it, and it turned out to be a refund for water bill charges Jim had been disputing for three years. He instructed Stella to deposit the check.

Stella sat down on the other side of the desk and began filling out a deposit slip. Beau, a cashier, came walking into Jim's office.

"Boss, there is a guy up here wanting to cash a thousand-dollar check. It's a check from Livingston Agricultural Consulting," the Newby explained.

"Cash it, that's Travis's side business. He's good for it," Jim ordered.

Beau left back down the hall. Stella was now licking the envelope containing the deposit.

"You want me to take it to the bank today?" she asked.

"No, I will take it in the morning when I make my rounds," Jim replied.

Stella left his office after Travis ordered her to check over everything and supervise the cashiers as they counted their drawers. With no further business needing his attention, he got up and informed his employees that he was going home for the day. He gave a few instructions to the incoming shift and walked out the door to his truck.

As he got to his truck, he stopped in his tracks as his ex-wife's attorney, Donald Willis, pulled in beside him.

"We've got to talk, Jim," he demanded in what seemed to Jim to be a drill sergeant's tone.

"No, we don't, and why the hell are you here anyway? The gas pumps are on the other side of the building," Jim responded in an equally harsh tone.

"This is serious, Jim. Christine's dad died last night, and you are the sole beneficiary in his will. He thought of you as a son, for a while anyway. He never changed it. He told me multiple times he wanted to change it, but he never did," Donald explained.

"I don't want it; send whatever documents I need to sign to Mike's office," Jim replied.

"Thank you, Jim. I knew you would be reasonable. I also knew that Mike was on vacation, and the executor of the estate is holding the reading of the will tomorrow. I was trying to help him get it straightened out," Donald explained.

"Send it to Mike's office. Once his secretary looks it over and gives the ok, I will sign it," Jim responded.

"Thanks again," Donald said.

"Eat shit," Jim retorted.

Even though Jim empathized with the man, he utterly despised Donald Willis, and he didn't mind if it showed.

CHAPTER 3

September 18, 2014

Edward Whitehorse woke before daylight. Everyone else at the camp was still asleep. He could hear the two big pale faces snoring. After four days of guiding six grown men around, he felt like a babysitter. Not one of the men he was guiding would be able to find their way around on their own. Lefty, who had been the nickname he had gone by since he was a child, started the fire, gathered his own gear, and mounted his horse to scout for the final hunting locations of the trip. The previous days had resulted in successful hunts, and everyone in the group had been enjoying themselves except Lefty. The men needed help with everything. They were rich oilfield men, yet all of their money had not enabled them to find deer on their own. It made Lefty laugh when they would ask him if he had feeders and food plots setup. Three days of tracking the deer and killing the deer the old-fashioned way had made Lefty's clients feel like real men. Even though that made Lefty somewhat happy because it meant he was doing a good job, it also made him sad. It made him realize he was part of a dying breed.

Lefty rode down the wooded hill where the group had camped the night before. He rode across a large meadow into a stand of pine trees. He dismounted and hobbled his horse. Continuing on foot, Lefty was looking for a group of persimmon trees where he knew that deer would be just after sunrise. He had two hours to get back to camp and get his clients into position. After emerging from the stand of pines, Lefty knew that the persimmon trees were about 300 yards away. He spent the next 30 minutes marking positions for his clients. He had to take great care where he placed his clients during a hunt, because on the first day of the hunt one of the "big ones" as Lefty called them shot at another member of the group. "I am glad that you were not blessed with marksmanship skills." Lefty had told the man at the time of the incident.

Satisfied with the hunter placements he had picked, Lefty began making his way back to the stand of pines where his horse waited. Lefty loved this time of the morning. It was still pitch-black dark, with a slight wind blowing through the trees. The world was not awake yet, and Lefty enjoyed the feeling that he was the only one moving around. It gave him a sense of superiority over nature, and a sense of calm that always made stress melt away. Lefty found his horse, removed the hobble from his feet, gathered the reins, and pulled himself into the saddle. When Lefty made his way back to the camp, he could still hear the big one's snoring. Lefty found a skillet and threw some bacon on. He knew the best way to wake up white men who had been out in the wilderness for four days was to start cooking. Soon after the smell began to permeate the area, men started waking up and migrating toward the fire. Lefty left them to their small feast and began packing up camp. After bellies were full and everybody was packed and ready, the small contingent of hunters made their way to the stand of pines where Lefty had been earlier in the morning.

Nobody said a word. Lefty had been very insistent that everybody in the group not utter a word during the time that made their way to the hunting locations. When the group made their way to the pine trees, they all dismounted, and Lefty took care of the horses. The group of hunters began pulling out their new fancy guns, as if the newer the gun was, the better the man. This always made Lefty wonder if these men would have been happier to spend four days in their houses showing of their gun collections. Lefty led the hunters to their positions and then returned to the pine trees. He spread out his bedroll and lay down for a nap. Lefty lay with his eyes closed, listening to the wind blow through the trees. This was his sanctuary, and he felt that these hills, mountains, and valleys were the kind of place he belonged to. A couple of hours later, Lefty was awakened by gunshots. He slowly rose when he could hear the pale faces giggling and moving through the woods so loudly that he knew why they couldn't kill a deer on their own. Lefty secured his bedroll to his saddle, gathered up the horses, and made his way to where he had heard the gunshot. He rode along, leading the horses with a feeling of contentment. The last hunt of the last day was almost over. Another round of giggling and movement could be heard, which signaled to Lefty that the pale faces had found their kill. It took lefty only 20 minutes to find the group gathered around the dead animal like a starving group of vultures fixing to devour their prey. They did not hear him come up behind them.

"What did we get this morning?" Lefty inquired.

"Jake got a big one, looks like the one we saw yesterday." One of the smaller white men said.

Lefty did not bother to learn anybody's name but Jake Patterson, who was the main client and also the one who would be paying Lefty for guiding the group on the hunt. The group had talked of "Indians" and their "crooked casinos" from the first day and Lefty had no desire to converse or learn anything about the men any more than he had to.

"I'm field dressing it now. I'll let John turn it in. I'm maxed out." Patterson said. Lefty had also noticed that these men talked in short, simple sentences all the time, and their simple speech patterns made Lefty feel amused. After the group sorted out how to report the kills of the trip, and with the horses loaded, the group made their way back to where they had left their trucks and horse trailers four days prior. As they approached what the locals called Snake Creek, Lefty knew that they were only 2 miles away from the area where their vehicles waited. The group of hunters was not aware of this because Lefty was leading the group back from a different direction than the way they departed. The hunters pulled up and set their horses along the creek as Lefty rode up beside Patterson.

"Now is the time that you pay me the other six hundred," Lefty said to Patterson.

"Yea, just call my secretary next week and she will send you a check." Patterson replied as he turned away from Lefty and began to ride across the creek.

"Our contract states that you were to pay me six hundred down, which you did, and another six hundred on the fourth day of the hunt.

It is now the fourth day, and I am requesting the remaining balance due," Lefty stated in a calm, cool voice.

Patterson was angered now, and he was unknowingly playing into Lefty's hands. Lefty had learned the hard way that if clients could find a way to slip away without paying him, they would. Since the early days, Lefty had devised a trick to ensure problem clients paid him.

"I said I will pay next week. Now that is that. Either take it or leave it," Patterson responded in a quick, angry voice. He was yelling now, and a small smile came across Lefty's face.

"No, I will just leave you," Lefty replied as he turned his horse, rode behind a group of cedar trees, and was gone.

Lefty loped his horse in a large circle around the group of hunters. He pulled up and sat his horse atop a knoll overlooking the group. He had ridden a large circle around the group, crossed Snake Creek a mile south of where the group sat, and had ridden to the top of the knoll. He watched the group.

"Fuck, Jake, what are we going to do now? We don't know where the hell we are," the other large man said to Patterson.

"I don't have any more food; we were supposed to be back at the truck in an hour," one of the smaller men said in a panic.

"Lefty! Lefty!" Patterson yelled.

With Patterson yelling, it seemed to put the others in a state of distress.

"Come back, hell, I will pay you!!" another man yelled. With his point made, Lefty slowly made his way down the knoll to where the group sat. He splashed into the creek behind the group, and from the opposite direction from which he departed. It startled the group, which drove home the point to the men that Lefty was the only one who knew how to get them out of there.

"I do not care from whom, but I want six hundred dollars, or I am going home," Lefty demanded.

Patterson pulled a roll of hundred-dollar bills from his pocket and handed them to Lefty. Lefty was looking at Patterson with eyes that could cut through wood, it seemed.

"We were just messing with you. Can you get us home now?" Patterson said as he laughed. He was trying to play the situation as less serious than it was. Patterson now knew that this was one Indian that he did not want to piss off.

"Let's go, pale faces," Lefty ordered as he began to lead the group back to their vehicles.

Four hours later, Lefty was pulling into Jim's station to fill his truck and grab something to eat. Jim saw him coming and met him at the gas pump.

"An oilfield bigwig just came in here, and he was complaining that a mean Comanche Indian left them stranded," Jim told him as he laughed.

"I did for about 25 minutes. Then they miraculously decided to pay me the money they owed me," Lefty responded with a big smile on his face.

"It's always the rich ones that try to skip out on the bill. Have you talked to Travis?" Jim said.

"He called me on the way over here. He said that he wanted us to go on a camping trip. Does that pale face not know that I just spent four days babysitting a group of white men out in the woods?" Lefty quipped as he chuckled.

"We are going to camp with camping trailers and maybe some fishing poles," Jim answered.

"In other words, we are going to camp like a bunch of weaklings. That sounds good to me," Lefty observed as he threw Jim a twenty-dollar bill for gas and got in his truck.

"You coming to Travis's house for steaks?" Lefty asked as he started his truck.

"Yes, I am. See you there," Jim responded as he turned and walked back toward the store.

Once he got back into the store, he turned and watched Lefty pull onto the highway and drive away. It always amazed him how Lefty always stayed two steps ahead of everybody around, and from what Patterson had told Stella earlier, it amazed Patterson, too.

As Jim pulled into his driveway, he stopped at his mailbox and exited his truck to check the mail. He removed the mail from the mailbox and thumbed through the envelopes. After concluding that it was all junk mail, he got back in his truck and looked upon the humble abode he called home.

It was a 1800 sq ft, three-bedroom, tan rock house that he designed himself. He loved the view of the house, which was set at the base of a large hill that was devoid of trees. The view from atop the hill was the sole reason Jim picked this place to build his house. He drove up to his house and shut off the engine. As he got out of his truck, his dog, "Forty," came wandering up. Forty was a half-blind cocker spaniel that came wandering up to his house one day about a year ago and stayed. Jim gave him some food and water, then went into his house.

He sat down on the couch and turned on the TV. He resumed his King of the Hill reruns that he had been watching earlier that day and sat back to relax. Jim was awakened sometime later by his cell phone ringing. "Hello," Jim answered. "Where the hell are you?" Travis demanded. "I'm at home. Why?" Jim responded. "Did you forget that you are due to make an appearance at my house?" Travis asked. "Yeap, I did. I'm on my way," Jim said and hung up. Twenty-five minutes later, Jim arrived at Travis's log cabin-style house and parked his truck beside Travis's and Lefty's in the circular driveway in front of the house. Jim opened the front door and stepped inside. He could hear voices coming from the back porch. He walked through the living room and stopped in the kitchen to look through the window into the backyard. He could see Lefty and Travis sitting at the outdoor kitchen bar. He walked out the back door, and Travis and Lefty turned around. "Ahh, there is Mr. Doom himself," Lefty said, chuckling. "Kiss my ass!" Jim said in response.

"I fell asleep watching TV. Travis woke me up when he called," Jim explained as he removed a Coors Light from an ice chest. "Me and this Comanche warrior have determined that a camping slash fishing slash beer drinking vacation is in our collective best interest," Travis explained in his usual overly complicated manner. "When?" Jim asked. "I'm free Monday, and Lefty is off next week," Travis responded. "I don't have to work; I have annual leave built up with the bingo tribe and I have no pale face guiding scheduled," Lefty added. "Well, I will have to put Stella and Rashad on management duty. I think I can make it work." Jim replied. "Listen to him, Lefty. He acts like he ain't the boss." Travis chided.

"Ok you got me; I wouldn't be doing any work at all even if I did go to work," Jim admitted.

"How's this going to go? Where are we going?" Jim asked Lefty.

"There is Blackstone Lake that nobody knows about, and there is also that lake that my aunt's friend owns three hours south of here, down by the Texas line," Lefty explained.

"Let's go south, far enough to keep Doom here from running back the first time his phone rings," Travis said.

"I'm fine with that. Lefty, what say you?" Jim said as he looked toward Lefty for a response.

"Good with me. I will call the old lady in the morning and tell her we are coming so she doesn't shoot us." Lefty said.

"Shoot us!?" Jim and Travis yelled in confusion at Lefty's reply.

"She doesn't like white people. She will shoot at us if I don't forewarn her." Lefty explained.

"I'll remind you to call her," Travis said as the group laughed.

The trio ate ribeye, drank beer, and laughed until past midnight. The men said their goodbyes and departed for their own houses, excited about the prospect of a relaxing vacation.

The next morning was a Friday, and Jim always checked in on his second store sometimes on Fridays or sometimes on Saturdays and Sundays. His preference was to make the trip on Sundays, but he usually went when time permitted. He had left his house at 630am and had almost arrived in the town of Helens when his phone rang. Jim answered, and Lefty said, "I have a question for the former accountant side of you. If I buy my own taser for my work with the bingo Indians, can I deduct it?" "No. Why are you calling me at seven am to ask me that?" Jim asked. "It just crossed my mind, and I figured the only Amish-like friend I have would probably be up." Lefty answered and then hung up without saying goodbye. Jim saw employees turning the lights on inside and sweeping. He entered the store without anybody noticing. "See, these are what floors are supposed to look like. Who was on duty last night?" Jim said to nobody in particular. "I was sir, and I got the overtime approved by Stella." A small 18-year-old boy said.

"Good job, Chase. You want to make some extra money this weekend?" Jim asked.

"Yea, I would like that. I'm saving for a car, so I'll take all I can get." Chase asked with obvious excitement.

"Go to my Bellville store and clean the floors, my office, and clean up the outside. Use the pressure washer on the building if it needs it. Rashad is on today and tomorrow. I'll tell him that you are in charge of all cleaning today and tomorrow." Jim ordered and began to walk away.

Chase was overwhelmed with the vote of confidence.

"Thanks, Boss, I, I..." Chase's words trailed off into silence.

"Get to work," Jim said with a grin on his face.

Chase grabbed his coat from behind the counter and ran out the door. Jim had hired Chase eight months earlier when he came into the store one hot July day, asking for work. Jim could tell by looking at him that day that he hadn't bathed or eaten in a while. Jim got him cleaned up and put him to work. In a couple of months, Chase was one of Jim's most reliable employees.

In his second store that sat just on the outside of a town called Helens, Jim had a computer and a stool behind the counter that sat off to the side of the main counter. From his perch, he could see the customers, but the customers couldn't see him. He got a cup of coffee, sat on his stool, and began to read the Tulsa World newspaper.

"Hey Jim, can I take off next Wednesday?" the cashier said.

"What you got going?" Jim inquired.

"I have to pick my brother up at the airport at 9. I was hoping to take off so he and I can play golf in Tulsa after he lands," the cashier said.

"Who works next Thursday?" Jim asked.

"Maria and Jake," the cashier said.

"Call Jake and see if he can work on Wednesday. If he can't, call Maria," Jim ordered, then went back to reading his paper.

The door chimed as a short, fat man with thick brown curly hair came in. Jim immediately recognized him as the man who had purchased the house out from under Travis. The man waddled back to the coffee and filled a large thermos. He then made his way to the chip isle and grabbed three large bags of Cool Ranch Doritos. He waddled back to the counter and placed his items on it. The cashier rang him up, the man paid, gathered his items, and began to waddle toward the front door. He paused and turned around.

"Excuse me, young man, but does Jim Blakely own this store?" the curly-headed man asked the cashier.

"Yes, I do," Jim replied before his cashier could answer. Jim stepped out from behind the area where his stool and computer were and emerged from behind the counter.

"Jim Blakely, what can I do for you?" Jim said as he extended his hand to the man.

The man shook Jim's hand and said, "My name is Dr. Robert Freeman. My realtor told me that Travis Livingston is a friend of yours. Do you know how I can get in touch with him? I need to talk to him," the man explained.

A big smile came across Jim's face. Dr. Freeman was talking. Jim pulled out his phone and dialed Travis's number. He picked up on the second ring.

"Hello there," Travis said.

"Curly-headed doctor wants to talk to you. Here he is." Jim said into the phone and immediately handed the phone to Dr. Freeman.

"Hello, sir, my name is Dr. Robert Freeman. We had a spirited conversation in my living room yesterday." Dr. Freeman explained.

"I have just received a very lucrative job offer in Durant, and I will be moving from the area. I would like to offer you first shot and buying my house." Dr Freeman said.

"Are you sure? But Mr. Livingston!" Dr Freeman said trying to hurry and get the words out.

He had a discouraged look on his face as he handed the phone back to Jim.

"Well, did you sell it?" Jim asked while trying not to laugh.

"He called me a curly-headed son of a bitch." Dr Freeman said as he handed the phone back to Jim. Dr. Freeman turned and exited the store. Jim laughed as he watched Dr. Freeman get into his car and drive away. It was days like this that made Jim love his job.

After 3 more hours at his stool, reconciling the bank account and going over inventory and double-checking the deposits from the previous day, Jim told the 3 employees working at the time that he would be gone all next week and that Stella and Rashad were in charge. They all wished him a good trip before he gathered his paper and coffee and walked out the door. Jim got into his truck as his phone began to ring. "Hello?" Jim said.

"Jim, it's Don Willis." The voice on the other end of the line said.

"What the hell do you want? I signed the papers so you could get Christine's dad's will straight." Jim demanded.

"The family wanted me to call and let you know how much they appreciate." Jim hung up without letting the man finish. His phone rang again, and he sent the call to voicemail. His phone rang again, and he was about to send it to voicemail again, but he noticed it was Lefty. "What's up, Lefty?" Jim asked. "I got all the arrangements made for our trip. We will leave on Sunday morning. We're pulling my camping trailer. Can you haul yours?" Lefty said.

"Yeap. I will have to check it over. The damn thing probably has four flat tires." Jim answered.

"Lefty, have you heard anything about Don Willis lately?" Jim asked.

"No, why?" Lefty asked.

"He just called me to thank me for signing some legal papers that helped him clean up a mess. It seemed odd for him to call me just to thank me. I think he's got something planned." Jim explained.

"You did know that he fired Christine from his client list, didn't you?" Lefty asked

"No! When did that happen?!" Jim asked. Jim was momentarily stunned. Fear began to make its presence known in his gut. Nothing good could come out of this, he thought.

"I heard from the security manager who was friends with her father that Christine wanted him to do some less-than-ethical legal work, and he fired her." Lefty told Jim as Jim wondered what the "less than legal" Work she wanted him to do was.

"I wonder what it was?" Jim asked. "Can you find out? I want to know if I am a potential victim of one of her crooked schemes."

"I will try. You want to ride with me to get food and stuff later?" Lefty asked.

"Sure, pick me up at the house later," Jim said.

"Ok, doomster, see you later," Lefty laughingly replied and hung up.

Jim sat there in his truck, racking his brain and mentally checking all his bases. He went over and over every detail of his divorce from Christine. There was nothing legal that she could do to cause him trouble, which worried Jim. He couldn't stand not knowing what she was up to. He made an attempt to summon all the patience within his body and managed to stay calm.

He removed the cell phone from his pocket and dialed Mike Prescott's cell phone number. It rang three times before Mike answered the phone.

"Prescott," a hurried voice answered.

"Mike, it's Jim Blakely. I have a situation that has just come up. I just got news about Christine, and I'm a little worried," Jim explained.

"What the hell has she done now?" Mike asked in a voice that was nicer and more concerned.

Jim explained what Lefty had told him.

"Hmmm," Mike sighed. "My guess would be that she asked Willis to forge a contract, or she asked him to file a frivolous lawsuit of some kind, or it could be a situation where she owes him money, and he lost his patience," Mike explained.

"See what you can find out, and then call me back. I'll pay you for your trouble, Mike," Jim requested.

"Sure thing. I'll do this little project pro bono. I'm on vacation, which means I have been spending time sitting on a bench while my wife spends more of my damn money. So I will be bored with time to kill. Buy me lunch when I get back in town, and we will call it even," Mike offered.

"Deal," Jim replied, and hung up.

CHAPTER 4

Jim headed left. Helens headed east toward Bellville. He listened to the slow blues licks of Albert King from the music on his cell phone. An avid blues fan, slow blues always soothed his nerves in times of uncertainty and stress.

As he approached the outskirts of Bellville, he cut north off the main highway toward his house. He stopped at the mailbox and checked for mail. There was nothing but junk mail, and Jim continued to his house. He pulled his truck in his garage and shut off the engine. He sat in his truck for a few moments, wondering what the hell his ex-wife could be up to.

He decided not to worry about it. Mike would call him back in a few days with information about whatever her scheme was, and he told himself that there was no sense worrying about it until then. He sat down on the couch when his cell phone rang.

"Hello." He answered.

"What in the hell is that crazy bitch of an ex-wife of yours up to now. It's all over town that Willis fired her ass." Travis demanded in his usual way of using too many useless words.

"Don't know. I just heard that from Lefty earlier today. Mike is going to see what he can find out." Jim explained.

"I wouldn't worry about it. She probably owes him money." Travis suggested.

"Could be. Lefty and I are going to go add to Walmart's bottom line after a while. Are you going to come along?" Jim asked.

"Nope, I already got my shit ready. You two are going to have to play catch-up by yourselves." Travis answered and hung up.

After Travis hung up, Jim eased into his couch, not planning on rising from his nest for several hours. The desire to turn on the TV didn't come as it usually did. Jim sat there, staring at the dark green walls and looking out the front window. The sun was starting to set, and the walls seemed to fade to black as the sun went down. He could see the mountains in the distance turn to a hazy blue as the light faded to darkness on the western horizon. Jim turned back to the blank TV in front of him. He still had no desire to hear anything, see anything, or listen to anything.

Jim reached for the laptop that sat next to him on the couch and powered it on. Jim opened his email and checked for new messages. There was an email from Mike Prescott.

It read: Jim, Judge Nelson called me and said that Joseph Eubanks, an attorney from Oklahoma City, has been retained as Christine's new attorney. She has adopted a 12-year-old girl, and there is a hearing next week. My secretary is emailing all the court documents that are public record. I will email or call you if anything of concern comes up.

Jim's mind remained somewhat blank after reading the email. Jim was confident that Mike would deal with it appropriately and keep him updated on anything that would concern him.

He got a paper and a pen and began to make a list of what he would need for the camping trip. Once he had a page and a half, he folded the list and put it in his pocket. He grabbed a beer from the fridge, sat on the couch, and waited for Lefty.

After about 45 minutes and 3 beers, Lefty walked through the front door.

"Are you ready to go buy a bunch of shit that we do not need?" Lefty asked.

"Primed and ready, boss, let's roll," Jim replied as he rose from the couch and headed toward the front door.

Fifteen minutes later, they were pulling into the Walmart parking lot. Lefty was always lucky enough to find a close spot, which always annoyed Jim.

"Every damn time." Jim quipped.

"Ahh Yeaahhh!!" Lefty hollered to drive the point home that he was luckier than Jim.

Jim laughed as he exited Lefty's truck. As the pair entered the store, they grabbed a shopping cart and headed into the madness of a rural Walmart.

"How much trouble is it for some of these stinkin' bastards to take a bath?!" Jim complained.

"You're at Walmart, Jim. This isn't exactly the best example of a customer base with good personal hygiene." Lefty explained. He was always serious and always seemed to find a logical explanation for whatever quandary he encountered.

Jim retrieved his own basket and separated from Lefty to find the items he needed. After 30 minutes of cussing, dodging people, and squinting at price tags, Jim was satisfied with his selection and headed for the checkout stands. As he entered the line and began waiting to check out, he could see Lefty standing by the door, with his items already bagged. Jim checked out, paid the cashier, and made his way over to where Lefty was waiting.

"About time." Lefty quipped as he pushed his cart toward the exit.

"Hey, once we're out there, you will be glad. I made sure I got everything I needed," Jim retorted.

The pair pushed their carts toward Lefty's green Chevrolet truck.

"Are you still a gambling man?" Lefty asked.

"Still," Jim replied.

"Paper, rock, scissors, Go!" Lefty said.

The two played paper, rock, scissors all the time to see who loaded all the items. Lefty lost when Jim's rock crushed his scissors.

"White man screwed me over again!" Lefty laughed as he began to load Jim's items.

As Lefty finished loading his and Jim's items into the truck, a car pulled up beside the truck, and a woman exited and walked toward Jim's side of the truck. The voice sounded familiar. Lefty walked around the truck to see what was going on.

Jim's ex-wife Christine was standing next to Jim's window, pointing a finger at Jim, yelling and cussing at the top of her lungs. Jim saw Lefty and immediately looked back at Christine.

"You pay me fifty thousand for screwing me over in the divorce, or I will sue you, then I'm going to fucking kill you!! You hear me! You have to do what I say now, you smug son of a bitch!!!" She demanded as Jim's face began to redden with anger.

Lefty made his way over to the driver's side of Christine's car, turned off the ignition, and popped the hood. Lefty calmly retrieved a multi-tool from his pocket, removed the battery, and closed the hood. Lefty put the battery under his arm and quickly walked over to the driver's side of his truck and got in. He set the battery in the seat next to him.

"Time to go!" Lefty said to Jim as he sat in the driver's seat.

Jim saw Lefty grab for the gear shift and quickly jumped in as the truck began to move.

"Thanks for getting me out of there quick; it was fixing to get ugly," Jim said as he put on his seatbelt.

"It was already ugly." Lefty retorted.

"But you have a bright side to the situation." Lefty offered with a small grin on his face.

"And that is?" Jim asked.

"The bitch will be walking home. Her car battery is sitting beside me." Lefty told Jim as he tried not to laugh.

Jim looked down into the seat and laughed out loud as he saw the car battery sitting in Lefty's seat beside him.

"The red man takes revenge quietly these days. I like it!" Jim said as the two sped off into the night.

Friday, September 19, 2014

The relentless, soul-scorching beam of light was burning through Jim's window when he awoke the next morning. It was 6 a.m., and he had to get all of his shit together for the camping trip, he thought to himself as he lay there. His mind kept going back to the night before to the encounter with Christine in the parking lot.

What in the world had gotten into her, he thought? She must have heard something that would lead her to believe that he had fifty thousand dollars that he could just spend any time he wanted.

He pushed it out of his mind and rose from his bed to get the day started.

A couple of hours later, he was backing his truck up to his camping trailer when he saw Travis's grey ford truck make its way up the driveway. He continued his task, and once he had the trailer hooked up, he began walking to his house to the place where the driveway ended into a parking area.

Travis waved as he got out of his truck and began to walk toward Jim.

"Ok Jim, it's Friday, bright and sunny, but if I were a betting man, I would bet that you could still find a way to coax something to bitch about from all this beauty that befalls us!" Travis prodded as he shook hands with Jim.

"Nothing about today necessarily, but I had a run-in with Christine last night," He responded.

"Ha Ha Ha, yeah, Lefty told me about it. That sneaky little bastard." Travis laughed.

"Oh well, I'm trying not to think about her. I'm ready to get away for a few days." Jim said.

"That's why I stopped by. I see you're getting ready; I'm going to go home and get my shit together and take it to Lefty's today. I just wanted to come by and see if you wanted to go get some breakfast, or shall I indulge on my own?" Travis explained.

"Well, might as well. Besides, I'm hungry, and I got more than enough time to get all my stuff done today." Jim replied as he began to walk to Travis's Truck.

A short time later, the pair pulled into the parking lot of the café. As they began walking toward the door, Travis said, "That's Don Willis's car in the parking lot. I'll hold him while you kick him in the nuts."

"I'll be fine as long as he doesn't try to talk to me," Jim responded.

They entered the café and sat down in a booth next to a window.

"Trav, why do you think Willis has been calling me a lot lately?" Jim asked.

"I don't know. Maybe he wants to tell you something, and he's trying to get on good terms with you first." Travis replied.

Jim began watching Willis. His blood began to rage as he watched him eat his breakfast and talk to his companions. Jim could feel the rage coming from deep within him, but as he always did, he pushed it back down, deep inside.

He calmed himself and brought himself out of his anger-driven trance by Travis's voice.

"You gonna order, or stare into the void like a Baptist who just found out they are allergic to casseroles?" Travis said laughingly.

"Turn two eggs over easy and slap a lot of crispy bacon on the plate as well," Jim told the waitress without taking his eyes off of Willis.

The wind began to blow outside. Pebbles could be heard hitting against the doors and windows as the wind began to blow dust up from the parking lot.

Jim hadn't said a word to Travis since they had sat down at the table. Travis kept looking at Jim as if to try to read his mind.

"You're thinking about her, aren't you?" Travis said.

"Yeap. Sometimes I can't help it. She's somebody else's problem now. It's just because Willis is here." He answered.

Travis leaned back in his chair as he began to speak.

"Well, it's like this. You got rid of a problem when you got rid of her. When you allow yourself to be, you're happy almost all day. This time of year, you get to acting a little like a grunge rocker who forgot to take his antidepressants, but most of the time, you're happy with your life. That's what you need to focus on." He explained.

"You're right, Trav. I'll try to allow myself to indulge in a somewhat happier disposition." He replied.

After their food arrived, they ate in silence. When they were done, Travis said that he would buy the meal. While Travis made his way to the cashier to pay, Jim walked outside to where Travis's truck was parked.

The wind blew dust and gravel everywhere, including in Jim's face. He jogged the rest of the way to the truck, opened the door, and got in.

"God Damn! Is it supposed to storm or something?" Travis asked as he struggled against the wind to close the truck door.

"Think so, later on tonight," Jim answered.

"I'll take you back to your humble abode. It's probably best that we all get our shit latched down and put away before the wind blows it all to hell, literally." Travis said as he waited for traffic to clear before pulling onto the highway.

A few minutes later, they arrived back at Jim's house.

"I can't get it out of my head, Trav. Why is that crooked bastard being nice to me? He has to know something or have something planned. Hell, I don't know." Jim said as he stared out the window.

"Well, it's not going to improve your life significantly by thinking about it every minute. Fuck it." Travis replied.

Jim exited Travis's truck, waved goodbye, and walked to his front door. He walked into the living room, sat on the couch, grabbed his laptop, and powered it on. He then logged into his email account.

There was a message from Mike Prescott. It read:

Jim, I think I have figured out what is going on. Christine is trying to adopt a distant cousin's daughter. Nothing for you to worry about. My guess is that Willis is trying to get into everybody's good graces since Christine is out of town now. The child has a trust fund and the whole family is after the money. I wouldn't worry about anything if I were you.

P.S. I want a ribeye for lunch.

Jim felt as if a thousand pounds had been lifted off of his shoulders when he read the email. He got off the couch, packed all his camping supplies into his camping trailer, then settled down on the couch to watch T.V. and drink a few beers.

Finally, Jim felt a sense of finality about his failed marriage. It felt as if he had closure, not as if in a bad ending, but it felt as if he had finally won in some sort of way.

He looked down at forty lying on the floor, looked at the dark green walls that he had chosen despite all of his friends' objections, and smiled. The familiar sound of a Coors Light bottle opening permeated the living room.

He turned on the TV and found an old British Comedy called "Are You Being Served?". He kicked his feet up and sat back for what felt like his first feeling of relaxation in years.

The storms rolled in that night just as Travis had predicted. Jim was still working on gathering his supplies for the trip. As he gathered the items and packed them into his camping trailer, a sense of contentment began to slowly intensify. He felt happy, completely content. Normally, when anything remotely close to a sense of contentment made its presence known in any way, shape, or form, Jim would immediately expect one hundred problems to be on the way to hit him at once. Today, however, the normal dread never manifested itself. Jim decided to take the happiness and forget that problems ever existed.

A few hours later, Jim settled down in his bedroom. As he turned onto his traditional left side sleeping position, he noticed that he had left his bathroom light on. He was so tired that he hardly noticed the beam of light shining directly into his eyes before he fell into a deep sleep.

Saturday, September 20, 2014

The unrelenting beam of sunshine woke Jim up the next morning. He raised himself to a sitting position on the side of the bed. He took a drink of water from the cup that was left on the nightstand the night before. He rose and walked the few steps it took to get to the window. Jim looked out the window. He could see the tops of the trees swaying in the wind. He could see the dew still on the grass. The tall pine trees that were scattered here and there stood like tall sentinels guarding the house. Jim could hear the wind as it whispered through the sky outside.

He stood there watching nature in its own element, undisturbed. He did not want to go outside. It would ruin the flow it seemed. He loved to watch nature. Lighting, a distant forest, swaying grass in a field, all seemed like the greatest of God's majesties to him.

Jim slowly woke himself from his nature-driven trance and made his way to the bathroom. He showered and shaved, then made his way to his closet. After dressing, he went to his dark green sanctuary and sat on the couch. He pulled on his boots, put Forty outside with plenty of food and water, and made his way to his waiting truck and travel trailer. He hadn't looked at his watch since he awoke. He glanced down at his watch and realized he was thirty minutes late. That thought had barely entered his head when his phone rang.

"If you would be so kind as to pull yourself from the immense joy of the dungeon you call home, would you please get your ass in gear?" Travis asked when Jim answered.

"On my way, Mr. Patience," Jim replied as he hung up the phone.

He glanced around at the trees and fields that lay in his view as he walked out his front door. The surrounding landscape seemed to be laid out to his disposal by some higher power. He felt attached to this land.

As he slowly walked to his truck, the unfamiliar feeling of contentment began to make its presence known. He didn't worry about karma coming around to get even. He submitted himself the feeling of happiness.

He opened his truck door as a smile spread across his face. He sat down in the driver's seat in his old truck, put it into gear, and drove down the driveway. As he slowed his truck and travel trailer to a stop at the stop sign below the hill from his house, he peered out at the winding stair mountains in the distance.

The past crossed his mind as always. He thought about Christine, and how he wondered if he would ever be happy, back when he walked out of the courthouse the day his divorce was final. It had taken what seemed like an eternity, but by the grace of God, happiness was at hand. As Jim pulled into Travis's driveway, he could see Lefty and Travis sitting on the front porch with numerous bottles sitting in each of their laps.

"What the fuck ?!" he said to himself.

He parked his truck directly behind Travis's truck, which was hooked to Lefty's travel trailer. He put his truck in park and grabbed his door handle.

He could hear Jim saying to Lefty, "You picked a hell of a time to get the shits! Hell, go eat a block of cheese that will plug you up."

He surmised that Lefty was not feeling well and that they were looking through Travis's inventory of medicine for a cure. He had put one foot on the ground and was about to put his other foot on the ground when he heard a sound that was reminiscent of a loud foghorn. Jim immediately looked toward the porch and saw Lefty giggling.

"God damnit! You nasty, shitty bastard! You just shit yourself!" Travis protested loudly as he waved his hand and trotted off the porch toward Jim's Truck.

Jim couldn't contain the laughter as he walked toward Jim. Jim stopped at the edge of the front yard in front of Travis's house.

"Lefty calling the Vikings?" Jim asked.

"Hell, he's probably got the bastards running here now! I think he's caught the fucking cholera. 150 years since the shitting sickness went through his tribe, and it makes a reappearance when we are trying to leave." Travis replied.

Travis turned toward Lefty, who was still laughing, and yelled, "You shit in my truck, and you will walk you stinkin' bastard!"

That comment made Lefty and Jim laugh that much harder. Lefty made his way to where Jim and Travis were standing and said, "You two ready to go, or should we stand here and bitch like a bunch of cackling women?"

"I'm waiting on Travis to regain his naturally calm composure," Jim responded.

"I'll calm down when he goes inside and wipes his ass!" Travis interjected.

After a couple of minutes of tense negotiations, a game of paper-rock-scissors, and several minutes of Travis bitching, it was decided that Lefty would ride with Travis. Jim would follow behind, riding solo.

Travis turned to Lefty as they walked to Travis's truck and proclaimed, "I hear so much as a mouse peep out of that stinkin' asshole of yours, you're riding with tight ass back there!"

"Deal," Lefty replied laughingly.

CHAPTER 5

The small caravan slowly made its way south toward their destination. They hadn't been on the road for an hour when, just north of Talihina, OK, Travis abruptly pulled to the side of the road, and Jim saw Lefty emerge from the truck and run to the travel trailer, open the door, and jump inside. Lefty emerged from the trailer wearing a different pair of pants. Lefty got back in Travis's truck just before Jim got a text message from Travis.

It read: "The strong, silent one caught a pain, and he almost made it to the shitter. Almost."

Jim laughed as he read the message. The day seemed to stand still, as if time were paused, as they drove south. He hadn't heard a word out of Travis or Lefty since Lefty had shit himself. He loved to drive with no hurried schedule awaiting him. The wind whistling past his window seemed to hypnotize him into another world. It was a world of no stress or worry.

Jim did not see how the trip that lay ahead could be more relaxing than the drive he was experiencing at that moment. He relished the sound of his truck roaring down the road, the sound of the wind, and the sight of the green wooded mountains. He had longed for the relaxation for a long, long time.

An hour further down the road, the group arrived at a small town called Clayton. Jim's phone beeped a text message alert. "The Indian is hungry, follow us." The message from Travis read. Shortly after, Lefty's blinker came on, and Jim followed him into the parking lot of a café.

Jim got out of his truck and walked between the front of his truck and the back of Lefty's trailer. He walked toward Lefty's truck and saw Travis open the door and get out of the truck. He bent halfway to a squatting position and let out what sounded like a tuba over loudspeakers.

"This man has no shame," said Lefty as he walked past Travis toward the café.

"Sounds like he is going to take a turn at shitting himself," Jim replied as he followed Lefty.

"Fuck both of you. A masculine creature such as myself needs to rear back and let it loose every once in a while," Travis exclaimed as he followed Jim and Lefty toward the café.

"Let yourself air out before you bring that shit in here," Jim said.

"I'll rid myself of the foulness before I enter," Travis quipped as he held the door open for Jim and Lefty.

"Table for three, please," Lefty told the waitress who was standing closest to the entry.

"Ya'll just sit anywhere you like," the waitress replied.

Lefty led the trio to an open booth in the corner of the restaurant. Jim took the gunfighter's seat while Lefty and Travis sat on each side.

"What are you eating, Jim?" Travis asked.

"Two eggs, over easy, with sausage and bacon," Jim responded as he closed the menu.

The trio sat at the table for what felt to them like an eternity. Lefty was the first one to break.

"Travis, do whatever the custom the whites do to get that piss ignorant bitch to bring us some coffee," Lefty ordered.

"Sure thing," Travis quipped as he hollered. "Tip in danger, coffee needed!"

"Damn," Jim thought to himself. A few minutes passed before the waitress came, bringing the group coffee.

"Tell me, how in the hell do you two stay civilized while I'm not with you?" Jim asked as he looked at Travis.

"We stay civil and mild-mannered most of the time, but I get pissy if I don't get my coffee," Travis replied.

The trio sat mostly in silence while they waited for their food. Once the food came, they all ate rather quickly, paid, and made their way back to their vehicles.

"Ya know, it seemed a bit more quiet than usual in there. Do ya'll have worries on your mind?" Jim asked as they walked through the parking lot to their trucks.

"Naaaww, Lefty is getting sleepy, it's his nap time. Now that I'm driving, we're gonna speed this bitch up a little bit," Travis replied.

"Good, I'd like to get there before we file for social security," Jim replied laughingly.

Lefty glared at the other two men, flipped off Jim and Travis, and said, "I drive safe!" as he climbed into the passenger seat of his truck and closed the door.

"I think we can make it the rest of the way without stopping. I got the address in the map thing on my phone. You good to go the rest of the way without stopping?" Travis asked Jim.

"Yeap, I'm good," Jim replied.

"Good, let's move this bitch on down the road," Travis said as he closed the truck door.

Jim made his way to his truck and followed Travis as he pulled onto the highway. Jim knew that they had about three hours left of driving, which would put them there with enough daylight left to get camp set up before dark. He relished three more hours of peace and quiet. The rest of the trip went by peacefully and uneventful.

At 4:45 pm, Travis turned into the driveway of a small house made of tan rock. The house sat about a quarter of a mile off the highway and was surrounded by about two acres of open field. Surrounding the house and open field was a forest. The place seemed like it was surrounded by huge walls of pine trees. Jim was mesmerized by the feeling of being surrounded by the formidable-looking natural barrier.

Lefty got out of the truck and walked up to the front door of the small rock house. Jim could see him knock on the door. A short time later, the door opened, and a small, old woman appeared. She looked pale and unhealthy, as if she hadn't been exposed to sunlight in years. After a short conversation, Jim saw the old woman give Lefty a key. Lefty then walked back to the truck and got in.

Jim's phone beeped a text message alert shortly after. Jim picked up his phone to read the message.

"Lefty got the key; the gate is down there at the tree line. Follow us," the message read.

Jim followed Travis and Lefty past the house and up to the gate, which was at the tree line directly behind the house. Lefty got out and opened the gate. Travis drove through, and Jim followed. Lefty shut and locked the gate after they both were through.

Lefty stopped at Jim's driver's side window on the way back to his truck.

"The lake is straight ahead. It's beautiful down there. Let's get out on the water before dark," Lefty said.

"With what? We didn't bring any damn boat!" Jim replied.

"There is a flat bottom at the campsite. It has a small motor. I brought everything I need to get the motor going," Lefty replied.

"I'm glad one of us came prepared," Jim said.

"Yeap. Look on the bright side. You may even survive this ordeal," Lefty said laughingly as he walked toward his truck.

Lefty got back into the truck, and their truck and trailer slowly began to roll forward. About an eighth of a mile down the path, the small caravan arrived at their destination. The lake was beautiful. It was remote, peaceful, and the water was perfectly calm.

The trio got their trailers set up and made a campfire. They all sat down around the fire a short time later. They were happy and content. The daily trials and tribulations of the real world seemed lifetimes away.

"Well, what ya'll think now? I'd say this peace and quiet was worth the effort of getting us and all of our shit here," Travis said.

"Yeah, it seems nice and calm. Phone calls and daily bullshit are gone," Jim replied.

Lefty had made his way to the edge of the water where the boat was. The water was beautiful. The campsite was on the shore of a large cove that opened up into a larger lake beyond. Jim sat and took in his surroundings. He loved the view of the large cove surrounded by tree-covered hills. He had longed for this kind of peaceful calm for years.

He then heard the sound of a small motor interrupt his thoughts. He looked down to the edge of the water and saw that Lefty had gotten the boat motor started.

"Grab the poles, you lazy white man, and get your ass in the boat!" Lefty hollered at Jim.

"Well, Lefty and I are going to see if we can't fuck up some fishing. Back later," Jim said to Travis as he grabbed fishing poles and walked toward the boat.

"Why don't ya'll try to catch something for us to eat!" Travis yelled back.

Lefty pushed the boat from the shore after Jim got in. The pair slowly made their way toward the mouth of the cove. They rode in silence until they were just a few yards short of the mouth.

"Let's try here first," Lefty said as he reached for his fishing pole. He had some homemade fishing lures.

"When did you become an engineer of fishing lures?" Jim asked Lefty, giggling at seeing his creation.

"I didn't. I just thought it looked cool," Lefty responded in his usual emotionless tone.

"Since I'm no fishing expert, I'm going to stick to my minnow and bobber. I'm craving some of that sac-au-lait, fried," Jim said as he cast his pole close to the shoreline.

"Whoever catches the first fish shall be immune from cleaning these sac-au-lait you speak of," Lefty proposed.

"Deal," Jim answered.

A few minutes later, Jim snagged the first fish. Lefty expressed the view that it was blind luck that resulted in Jim catching the first fish. The two fished in silence for almost an hour until darkness started to set in.

"Lefty, what do you think about it? You glad to be here?" Jim inquired of his companion.

"Yea, I needed a break. All the assholes who work so hard to keep from paying you,that is what I hate about doing business with people," Lefty responded.

"That's part of running your own gig. Everybody wants something for free," Jim agreed.

"Lefty, do you ever wonder if you made the right choice in life? I mean, do you ever wonder what would have happened if you had chosen something else at a critical juncture in the past?" Jim asked his friend.

"Jim, you did the right thing when you divorced Christine. I know that's what you're really asking about," Lefty replied without hesitation. With a simple comment, Lefty had eased Jim's mind. Jim was always envious of Lefty's simple way of looking at situations. That way of thinking almost always resulted in Lefty leaving all situations feeling content and happy. Jim was never that lucky.

"Saw right through me on that one, didn't you?" Jim asked laughingly.

"Yeap. Anytime it gets quiet, your mind wanders to crazy women," Lefty responded.

The two talked about old times and shot the breeze until it was almost too dark to fish. Then Lefty started the boat, and they made their way back to shore. As they got close to shore, they could see that Travis was asleep in a lawn chair next to a small campfire.

"Ooooh. Lefty makes white men scared!" Lefty whispered to Jim as he tried not to laugh.

They pulled the boat onto shore and slowly snuck up to where Travis was asleep. Lefty pulled a small .22 pistol from his belt and fired three shots into the air. Travis's eyes opened wide, and he shot to his feet and began to sprint away.

"Where are you going?" Lefty asked as he and Jim laughed hysterically.

"You son of a bitch! I just damn near pissed myself. I'm not sure what was moving faster, my legs or my fucking blood pressure!" Travis exclaimed.

"Trav, you were hauling ass to somewhere!" Jim said as he continued to hee-haw.

"Fuck both of you. You know, revenge is a bitch. Ya'll remember that when I get you back!" Travis vowed.

After the laughter died down, the trio feasted on fish fried over a campfire. They ate until they were so full they were almost sick from eating too much.

With bellies full, sleep began to take priority. Travis and Lefty migrated to Lefty's trailer. Jim sat alone at the campfire. He listened to the fire crackle. He saw the moonlight dancing across the water of the lake. He heard the wind send a low whistle into the night through the trees. This was exactly what he needed.

CHAPTER 6

The next morning, Jim slept in until 10:00 am. He slowly rose out of bed and got dressed. He made his way out of the camper to meet the morning. It was peaceful, calm, and pristine. He stood there for a moment, taking in the morning. He could see the sunlight dancing on the water, hear the wind blowing through the trees. The peacefulness he had needed for a long time now. He didn't see Travis or Lefty anywhere. The boat was gone, so he assumed they were out fishing. He got binoculars out of Travis's truck and gazed out over the water. He could spot the boat way out on the water beyond the mouth of the cove.

Jim went back into his camping trailer and lay down on his bed for more rest. When Jim awoke again, it was almost dark. He grabbed a lawn chair and sat beside the water. He rigged a pole with a minnow and a bobber and cast out in the water. The bobber went under after a few minutes, and Jim reeled in a crappie that weighed about a half pound. He grabbed the fish and held it up.

"There's one!" he said to himself and got up to put the fish on the stringer.

He felt a stinging pain in the back of his head. He dropped to his knees. He lost his grip on the fish, and it flopped back into the water. Jim tried to turn his head, and that's when it all went black.

"Lefty, it is a shame to see how far you have fallen off of the mantle of fishing champions!" Travis chided.

"You have caught one more fish than me! I understand how little experience you have with the sensation of winning anything," Lefty calmly replied.

Travis could hear something pop, followed by a faint sound of laughing.

"You hear that?" Travis asked as he looked back toward the campsite.

"Not walking into that one, pale face," Lefty replied.

"No, goddamnit! I hear people laughing, and I heard something go 'pop' back toward the campsite," Travis explained.

Lefty peered hard toward the campsite. Travis looked at Lefty, because Lefty could see twice as good as Travis could hear, and Travis could hear anything. It was nearing dark, so it was hard to see from where they were. Lefty looked toward camp and said nothing for a couple of minutes.

"I see three people. Can't tell who they are," Lefty said.

Travis lost color in his face.

"Left, what the hell are you talking about, three people?" Travis asked as panic rose inside him.

"There are three people at the camp I could see," Lefty explained.

Travis peered hard toward the campsite and strained to see what was going on.

"What the hell are they doing? Can you see what they are doing?" Travis asked Lefty with rising concern in his voice.

"I can't see for sure. Let's ease closer to camp to where we can see," Lefty responded.

Lefty guided the boat along the bank at a slow pace, avoiding heading directly at the camp in an effort to keep from being too obvious. They made their way about 100 yards closer.

"Two people I don't know. I see Jim lying on the ground," Lefty said, maintaining his cool.

"On the ground? What the fuck?" Travis said in a state of confusion.

"What the hell is he lying down for?" Travis asked.

"I don't know."

Lefty's voice trailed off as both he and Travis saw one of the strangers kick Jim in the stomach while Jim was lying on the ground.

"Oh my god," Travis said.

"No, god will more than likely be mad at me for what I am about to do," Lefty said while still maintaining his composure.

"Travis, drive. Hand me that .22. Now!" Lefty ordered.

Travis complied with Lefty's request without question and swapped seats with Lefty after handing him the .22 rifle they had with them. They saw Jim try to rise to his knees when the same stranger kicked him in the stomach again.

At this point, they were within about 250 yards of the camp, while still staying close to shore, approaching from the far-left side of the camp, and would not be visible until they were within 40 yards of the camp. The pair said nothing during the last 200 yards of the trip.

Finally, Lefty said, "I'm not going to ask any fucking questions, I'm going to shoot that son of a bitch."

"Lefty! Hold on now! Once they see a gun on them, surely they will either run off or stop to see what is going on! It's murder if we shoot them in the god damned back!" Travis pleaded.

"They will have a chance, but just one, and it won't last long," Lefty calmly replied.

Travis's mind was in a panic. He knew that Lefty was a crack shot and that he would kill the men without hesitation if they provoked him.

The light from Jim's camper illuminated the front of the boat as the boat came into view of the camp. Lefty shouldered the rifle and yelled, "One more fucking move, and I will make your asshole spout shit!"

"Who the fuck?" a large man in an orange camouflage ball cap said as he wheeled away from Jim and looked toward the boat.

"Get outta here or we'll fucking kill you! Mind your own fucking business!" a slightly smaller stranger said in a strong hick accent. As he talked, he pulled up a pistol and pointed it toward the boat.

The report of a rifle rang out across the water as Lefty fired. The smaller stranger fell backward as the bullet struck him in the sternum. The large stranger immediately fell to his knees and put his hands in the air.

"Don't kill me! Please don't kill me! I'm unarmed!" the larger stranger yelled, his voice breaking under the fear of seeing his friend shot and killed before his eyes.

Lefty stepped out of the boat and waded the final ten feet to shore. Travis hopped out of the boat and pulled the front part of the boat onto shore, then followed behind Lefty.

Travis went straight to Jim.

"Jim! Jim! Are you ok?" Travis asked frantically.

"I think I got a couple of broken ribs and bruised pretty bad, but I'll live," Jim replied, straining to talk through the pain.

Meanwhile, Lefty put the barrel of the rifle to the large stranger's head and said,

"Start talking."

"That's my cousin you just killed!" the large man said.

"Wrong answer!" Lefty yelled as he hit the large man in the stomach with the butt of the rifle. The large man fell forward onto his face but raised back up onto his knees after a few moments. He clutched his stomach in pain.

"We live down the road from the old woman. We heard there were some people down here from out of town with a couple of nice campers. We came down here to steal one of them. We got a drug debt, man; it was either steal them or worse people than us would kill my cousin and me!" the large man said, fighting back tears.

"I can't believe it turned out like this. Fuck this! My life is over!!" the large man said. The man was sobbing now.

"Stay on your knees. Put your hands straight up in the fucking air," Lefty ordered.

"Travis, find a rope or something," Lefty ordered.

Travis went into Lefty's trailer. He emerged a couple of minutes later with some white nylon rope. Travis moved the stranger's hands behind his back and tied them together.

"Oh my god, that's too tight!" the stranger cried.

"Deal with it, princess!" Travis responded. Travis stood back and looked at Lefty.

"What do we do now?" Travis asked while still breathing hard.

"We need to get a hold of the police. Try your cell phone," Lefty replied.

"Here, use mine. It has service," Jim said, holding up his cell phone.

Travis went over to where Jim was still doubled over on the ground and grabbed the phone. He dialed 911 and waited.

"Emergency services, what is your emergency?" a woman's voice said.

"There has been an attempted robbery. Two robbers attempted to rob us, and one of them pulled a gun. My friend returned fire and killed one of the robbers in self-defense. We need police here fast!" Travis explained while trying to remain calm.

"Is any of your party hurt?" the woman asked.

"They beat up my friend pretty badly. There are three of us. Two robbers, and one of them is dead. We are at Blackstone Lake behind..." Travis stopped talking as the woman interrupted him.

"We can track your phone, sir. Stay with me until I get a location on you," the woman ordered.

"Ok," Travis replied.

"What is the condition of the robber that is still alive?" the woman asked.

"He is on his knees with his hands tied behind his back, with a full-blood Comanche holding him at gunpoint," Travis explained.

The woman continued to ask questions about what happened and inquired about Jim's condition. About 15 minutes later, Travis could hear sirens.

"I hear sirens coming," Travis told the woman.

"Ok, stay with me until they get there," the woman said.

Lefty kept both eyes on the large stranger as he listened to Travis talk on the phone. He could also hear the sirens getting closer. Then he could see the lights passing the house and started to head to their camp. There was only one SUV with flashing lights pulling up behind Jim's trailer.

An officer exited the SUV and jogged toward Lefty as the officer pulled his weapon.

"I got him, sir. Put the rifle down!" the officer yelled at Lefty.

Lefty backed away from the stranger a few steps and slowly put the rifle on the ground.

"Good, good," the officer said as he stepped behind the stranger and handcuffed him. The officer retrieved a pocketknife from his pocket and cut away the rope that Travis had tied around the stranger's hands. He then holstered his weapon and went over to Jim and looked toward Lefty.

"If he moves, you can pick up your rifle and shoot the bastard," the officer told Lefty.

After checking on Jim, the officer walked back over to where Lefty was and asked which one of them had called 911, as two more police vehicles and an ambulance arrived. Travis told them that he did and began telling the officer what happened.

More officers arrived and began to take statements from all three. After listening to Travis, Jim, and Lefty tell what happened for what seemed like 50 times, they loaded Jim into the ambulance and took him to the hospital.

Lefty and Travis stood there in silence. They watched the police finish up their note-taking and handcuffing, and the crowd of flashing lights began to slowly dissipate.

"Left, what do we do now? For the first time in my life, I'm at a loss for words."

"I don't know. It all happened so fucking fast. It was a normal day a couple of hours ago. I don't understand how, or why," Lefty's words trailed into silence as the shock of what happened took hold over both him and Travis.

"Let's go find out where they are taking Jim before the damn ambulance leaves," Travis suggested as the two began walking to the ambulance. By this time, the ambulance and one police SUV were the only remaining emergency vehicles still there.

Jim was sitting up on the stretcher in the back of the ambulance. He looked down and saw Travis and Lefty.

"Well, I'm still alive. Concussion, they say," Jim said as a paramedic helped him to lie down on the stretcher.

"Where are they taking you?" Travis asked.

"Antlers. I don't know the name of the hospital, but I'm guessing it's probably the only one there," Jim replied.

"Ok, we will load up the convoy here and head that way. Jim, you will be there by yourself for about an hour. It will take us at least that long to gather all of our shit up," Travis explained.

"I'll be fine. Take your time. They will probably be running tests for a while anyway. See you two crazy bastards later," Jim replied with a smile as he closed his eyes and dozed off to sleep.

He woke up sometime later in a hospital room.

"Where am I?" he asked.

"Pushmataha Hospital in Antlers," a young nurse answered.

"Oh, ok. Do I have to stay awake?" Jim asked.

"No, sir, we are going to run some tests. We will wake you up when we are done," the nurse told him.

Jim closed his eyes and went back to sleep. When Jim woke up again, he was still in the same hospital room. Travis and Lefty were standing at the end of the bed, staring at him.

"Well, you gonna live?" Travis asked.

"Haven't been told any different," Jim replied.

A doctor of what looked like Arab descent walked in.

"Hello, Mr. Blakely, I am Doctor Amari. We have done some imaging, among some other tests, and we can conclude that you have had a mild concussion. You will be fine in a few days. You may experience some headaches, dizziness, and fatigue for a few days, and that will be completely normal," the doctor explained. The doctor finished explaining using terms that Jim did not understand. He gave Jim a prescription and told him to follow up with his primary care doctor.

After waiting another 30 minutes for discharge papers, Jim put on his shoes as his two friends needled him.

"Hell, he will probably need a wheelchair," Travis said, laughing.

"Jim, you will probably need a cane at least," Lefty chimed in.

"Listen, assholes, I got hit in the head, I'm not going to a goddamn nursing home," Jim shot back.

The trio laughed as they walked out of the room.

"Jim, I'm driving your rig. I guess you can pick who you ride home with," Lefty said.

"Oh god, I'm riding with you, Left. I know of a certain someone who isn't known to be quiet for any length of time," Jim replied.

"Now ya'll can kiss my ass. Just because I like to say more than five words during each day, I'm a loudmouth. I just think both of ya'll are jealous of my superior vocabulary," Travis replied, smiling.

"Travis, about seventy-five percent of those words were unnecessary," Jim explained.

The trio laughed as they walked out of the hospital. Jim crawled up into the passenger seat of his truck as Lefty climbed into the driver's seat.

Jim slept almost all the way home. A few miles from their hometown, Jim woke up.

"Damn, was I out the whole way home?" Jim asked.

"Yeap, and you fucking snore," Lefty replied.

"I'm going to drop you off at home. I'll unhook all your shit for you. You go lie down and rest," Lefty said to Jim as Jim raised his seat up and looked out the window.

"How are you, Left? Don't tell me you're fine. You shot and killed a man. I know you had to. You saved all of our lives, not to mention your own," Jim stayed his gaze on Lefty as he waited for a response.

"I know I would be dead if I didn't shoot that son of a bitch," Lefty took a deep breath as he continued. "I can't forget his eyes. The look of complete fear and total surprise in his eyes, I keep thinking that he knew he was fixing to be sent to hell in short order. That absolute fear must have shot through his veins. I prayed to the creator the whole way home that I wish I could have shot that fear through him instead of a bullet."

That left Jim speechless.

"I don't know what to say. Do you want me to stay here with you and hang out? Are you going to be okay?" Jim asked. Jim was worried about Lefty. He had never seen worry manifest itself in someone's eyes like it was now.

"I'll be okay. I just need some time to myself. I will call you tomorrow. I will feel better by then," Lefty replied.

A few minutes later, they were driving up Jim's driveway.

"Who the hell is that?" Lefty asked as he nudged Jim to get him to look and see who was in Jim's front yard.

Jim squinted and said, "That's Rashad mowing, and Stella sweeping the porch. How the hell did they find out what was going on?"

"I'm sure it's all over hell and half of Georgia by now," Lefty replied calmly.

Lefty backed the trailer in its place and then helped Jim out of the truck and onto the front porch.

"All right, what are ya'll doing here?" Jim asked as he sat in a chair on the porch.

"We heard about what happened when the police were getting gas. We came up here to check on you yesterday, but you weren't here. We thought we may do some chores so you could take it easy. I also did the schedule for both stores, and we calculated the deposits and put them on your kitchen table. If you need us to take them to the bank, just let me know," Stella replied.

Jim wanted to be mad at the pair for going in his house without him knowing, but he knew that what they did was commendable. They didn't have to come check on him, and they damn sure didn't have to help get the yard mowed and the house straightened up. Jim decided that he was grateful.

"I appreciate what ya'll have done. I'll be fine. We're all a lot more shook up and shocked than we are hurt," Jim said.

"Ya'll can go on home now; I'll manage," Jim told them. They told him to call if they needed anything, and he almost sent them to the liquor store, but he decided against the idea.

After Lefty unhooked the trailer and parked Jim's truck, he walked onto the porch and sat in the lawn chair beside Jim.

"Well, fuck," he said.

"Yeah, what the hell do we do now?" Jim asked.

"Short term, I'm going to go check on Travis, then take my ass to bed," Lefty explained.

"I've never been this tired," Jim said.

"Call me tomorrow and let me know you're okay, Lefty," Jim told him.

"I will, don't worry. It will all be okay," Lefty replied. Jim was not sure that would ring true.

The next day, the incident was all over the local radio stations and was being reported on the regional TV networks. Stella had texted him at 6:30 that morning, saying there were two TV vans filling up with gas at the station.

At about 9:00, Jim called his attorney, Mike Prescott.

"This is Mike," a voice answered.

"Hey Mike, it's me, Jim," Jim said.

"Hey Jim! What the hell did you all get into down there? I heard about it on the radio this morning," Mike asked.

"A robbery gone bad. Lefty shot and killed one of the robbers when they were trying to raise a gun and shoot him," Jim added.

"What do I tell the media? I heard there are a couple of TV crews in town," Jim asked.

"Tell them no comment. Do you want me to release a statement to the media? It will get reporters referring questions to my office instead of hounding you. I can get Sarah on it; she is good at that kind of thing," Mike suggested.

"Sounds like that will be best. Thank you, Mike. Let me know if you need anything from me," Jim replied.

"Will do. This should all blow over in a couple of days,the media frenzy, that is. I'll call you tomorrow," Mike said and then hung up.

The next morning, it would all change.

CHAPTER 7

The pulsing buzz of an alarm clock rang out in the early morning hours like the boom of thunder disturbing a virgin earth. The dark-haired woman opened her eyes, annoyed to be disturbed from her nightly hibernation. She reached over to her phone and silenced the alarm to begin her morning waking-up routine. After rising from the bed, she rolled out a yoga mat and turned on her relax playlist from her YouTube Music app. With 30 minutes of yoga completed, she rolled her yoga mat back up, stowed it away, and made her way into the shower. After another hour, she was all made up into her regular gorgeous self. She still considered herself a knockout even at 38 and knew how to use that fact to her full advantage. She took one last glance at the clock. It was 4:30 am. She still had an hour to get to where she was going.

A forty-six-minute drive brought her to the Circle Cinema on Lewis Avenue in Tulsa. The man said to meet him just inside the front door at 5:30 am. She parked her car several blocks away along the street so that it would not be seen at the theater. She walked up to the front door and tried it. It opened. She walked inside and heard a deep, gravely male voice. "You're early, you sure you've never done this before?" The man said. "No, I haven't." She replied in a voice a little shakier than normal. She didn't know where the man was, and it took a significant amount of willpower to keep herself from looking frantically around the room to try to find the man. A small lamp came on. The lamp was sitting on a plastic picnic table about 30 feet inside the front door. She still did not see the man. She could make out a plastic folding chair beside the table. "Sit down at the table." The man said. She forced herself to stay calm and walked over to the chair and sat down. "That's better. Now show me the inside of your pockets. "He ordered. She complied. "Good. Now we will see how serious you are. I have no idea if you are wearing a wire or have a weapon. So, for this to go forward, you're going to take off all your clothes, spin all the way around, and let me see for sure that you're clean." The man ordered in a calm but determined voice. Christine had not anticipated this. She thought rapidly to herself. "Was he some kind of pervert? Were there other people in here? Or was she even on video?" she asked herself. She decided that she had come this far and decided to go forward. She stood up, pulled her shoes off, followed by her pants, shirt, and her undergarments. At first, she crossed her arms over her breasts to hide them. "Let me fucking see them." The man growled. She dropped her hands. "OK. Sit down." He ordered. "Now, you want your ex-beau knocked off?" The man asked. "Yes, I'm going to be broke and out on my ass if I don't collect the life insurance policy I have on him." She answered. "Does he know that you have a life insurance policy on him?" The man asked. "No, I took it out on him when we were married and paid the premiums from my own account so that he wouldn't know." She explained. "Alright, here's the deal. You only got eighteen grand saved. Isn't that what you told me?" The man asked. "That's right," Christine replied. "Ok, then here's what you've got to do. I'm not an unreasonable man, so you give me ten grand, and I'll loan you the other forty, with interest, of course. Let's say twenty percent. You can pay me when you collect the life insurance. If you don't collect for a problem with the insurance, fuck you, pay me. That being said, if one of my guys fucks up, then you're still out the ten grand, but you don't have to pay me the forty." The man said as Christine could hear the sound of someone pacing around the room. "Ok, that sounds fair, I agree." She agreed. It was the same terms that she had been told would be offered, and she was glad there were no surprises. Well, almost no surprises, other than sitting butt naked on a chair in a lobby of an obscure theater. "Good." The man said, drawing the word out to show that he was glad she agreed. "Now, for the last thing. We don't seal the deal with you on a handshake around here; that's only for men." The man said as he walked into the lamplight. He was about five ten, with salt and pepper hair and a short beard. Christine knew what he meant and complied with the final obligation.

After spending a whole day at home doing nothing, Jim rose from his bed the next day, determined to keep a normal schedule. He did not sit well. He couldn't stand to sit around and do nothing. He showered, shaved, and got dressed. As he walked down the hall to the living room, he looked to the place where he normally kept a couple of pairs of shoes handy and did not see anything. "God Damnit. Now I'm going to have to go on a fucking scavenger hunt to find shoes." Jim cursed to himself. He looked all around, in his closets, under the bed, and in every nook and cranny in the living room. He conceded defeat and called Stella on the phone.

"Hey, Boss! How are you feeling?" She answered in a cheery voice. Jim was fixing to dampen that mood significantly. "Where the hell are my shoes? I've looked all over this place, and I'm becoming convinced that I will be going sock foot all day." Jim said while trying not to yell.

"They are in the kitchen under the table." She answered.

Jim was so annoyed at the unique choice of place to store his shoes that he hung up. He dragged his boots from underneath the table and pulled them on. He started over. He was trying to leave the house in a good mood, and it wasn't working out. He stood quietly and cleared his mind. "Ok. Let's do this." Jim encouraged himself as he walked out the door.

Travis woke up early that morning after tossing and turning all night. In significant contrast to his interaction with other humans, Travis rarely talked to himself when he was alone. The experience had left him shaken, as it would anyone. After he got out of bed and dressed himself, Travis made his way to his kitchen and started a pot of coffee. He had to go to the livestock sale in Ft Smith and purchase 30 heifers for a customer. Travis had built a reputation in the cattle business as a keen evaluator of cattle. His customers came to him because, more often than not, Travis got them good, quality, healthy cattle that did well. When Travis moved to the area, he owned a hardware store and had a large herd of cattle of his own. He noticed a lot of people in the area were relatively young, with jobs, and did not have the time to go to each cattle sale to get the cream of the crop. Travis made his own little industry here, and both he and his customers were happy. Travis would get calls from his customers that needed cows, bulls, yearlings, heifers, you name it. Travis would purchase the cattle for the customer, and make sure they were hauled to the customer. He made sure his fee was well worth the service he provided.

He stood in his kitchen drinking coffee. He dreaded the day, but he knew work had to be done, and he headed out the door. Once he arrived at the Ft Smith Livestock Auction and walked to his normal seat. All the other men there at first looked shocked and surprised to see him. Many of them came over to him and told him they were glad he was ok, and many of them very quickly offered to buy cattle for his customers if he didn't feel up to it just yet. "Contrary to your opinion, I'm fixing to take the best heifers here with me, and I don't need your help, especially since your glasses are as thick as your wife," Jim told one of the regulars at the auction. They both had a laugh, and it seemed to everyone that Travis was his old self. Travis, however, did not feel like his normal self and knew he would never be the same. After 3 hours, Jim had half of the heifers; he needed to fill his customer's request. A group of seven good-looking black heifers came into the ring. Travis put in his bid. Some asshole kept bidding them up higher. Travis raised the bidding by another fifteen cents a pound, then quit. "Damn, Trav, I thought you were serious on that one." The guy sitting next to Travis said. "I'm just spending some of that son of bitch down there's money," Travis explained. Travis knew that the less money the gentlemen in the front row had in their pockets, the cheaper these cattle would go for later on in the morning. Travis's strategy worked, as an hour and a half later, the gentlemen left, shooting dirty looks at Travis while he walked toward the exit. Travis purchased the rest of the heifers he needed in relatively short order. He left the auction area and walked into the lobby. After paying for the cattle and arranging for delivery, he called his customer.

"Jake, you pot-bellied alcoholic, I got your beef," Jake said when the man answered.

"Damn already? I figured it may take a couple of weeks to find thirty that were top-notch from what I've seen go through the sales lately." The man replied.

"That's why I'm able to stay clothed and living indoors. God help me if there were no cattlemen or cattle." Jim replied.

"God would have to help us all if there were not cattlemen or cows," The man replied. "Text me the total, and I will leave a check in the usual spot." The man explained.

"Thanks, Jake," Travis said and then hung up. Travis walked out to his truck in a good mood.

That same afternoon, Lefty went into work for his shift. His supervisor wanted him to start out with half shifts for a couple of days before so that Lefty could work back into the swing of things. Lefty always viewed his job as the easiest job in the world. Nothing much ever happened other than the occasional drunk getting too rowdy and the occasional fight between the gamblers. Lefty had always struggled with determining what his purpose in life was. His heart wasn't in his current job, and he had no clue what his dream job was. Since he had moved to the Choctaw Nation part of Oklahoma from the Numunuu lands where he grew up, he had struggled to find purpose in his life. It wasn't his choice to leave the Numunuu or Comanche, Lands was not his choice. Lefty had punched a state senator's son in a bar in Lawton, OK. The guy had been taunting Lefty all night, and when the man grabbed the rear end of one of Lefty's female friends, Lefty unloaded on the asshole with a right hook to the face. The man's father, the state senator, was good friends with the district attorney. A local attorney, with whom Lefty was friends, had a long heart-to-heart talk with Lefty, and they decided that Lefty's best choice was to get the hell out of Dodge, so to speak. One of Lefty's friends was on the Numunuu tribal council and helped Lefty get a job working as a security manager over a few of the Choctaw casinos. That was how Lefty got to southeastern Oklahoma. At the end of his shift, Lefty clocked out and walked to his truck in the parking lot. It was 530 in the afternoon, and he was beat. He decided to stop by Travis's on the way home. He needed someone to talk to, and Travis's favorite thing to do was to engage in conversation.

Travis was passed out asleep when Lefty arrived at his front door. He retrieved the spare key from a key slot hidden under the railing on Travis's front porch and opened the door. He quietly replaced the key in its original hiding spot and strode toward the sound of snoring. He shook Travis to wake him and sat down in a recliner beside the couch where Travis was sleeping. Travis slowly rose from his slumber, got up, and walked down the hall toward the bathroom without looking around. When he walked back into the living room, he noticed Lefty and jumped sideways. It scared him so bad. "God Damnit! You scared the holy living dog shit out of me! You're trying to give me a fucking stroke!!" Travis yelled. Lefty giggled quietly

"Now help me find my fuckin' blood pressure medicine," Travis ordered.

"Sit down, white man, I need to talk to someone," Lefty explained

"What?!" Travis asked, surprised. "You never in your life have uttered one word that wasn't absolutely necessary to your continued existence?" Travis offered further.

"Shooting that guy has got me messed up a little still," Lefty said. "I know that I had to, and the guy left me no choice. But I can't get that look he had on his face right after the bullet hit him out of my head." Lefty explained while Travis walked around the room searching for his blood pressure medicine. "Well, my friend, I think in your situation it would do you some good to consider what your alternative would have looked like. If you hadn't shot him, you would be dead. We know that for sure. I know that doesn't make rainbows and sunshine sprout out of your ass automatically, but it should give you some sense of peace knowing that it was either that thieving son of a bitch or you. You chose to stand up to a thief who was trying to kill you. It was pretty damn admirable if you ask me." Travis said he found his blood pressure medicine and sat back down on the couch.

"Don't keep beating yourself up over this. You have to let yourself heal from this. Let yourself try to start feeling happy again." Travis said.

"I'll give all that a try. I started working again. Just half shifts for the first couple of days until Friday. That will be my first full shift back." Lefty replied.

"Then Friday night, let's get the grand trio of travelers together for the consumption of steak and a few beers," Travis suggested.

"What's today? Wednesday? Yeah, that sounds good to me. I'll call Jim when I get home." Lefty replied.

Travis swallowed his pills and turned to Lefty and said, " Ya know, you probably saved a few lives by killing that motherfucker."

"You are most likely correct," Lefty replied.

"Fuck em'. They can kiss my skinny white ass. I'm sure we will all have to go testify at that one's trial." Travis surmised.

"Yeah. Thanks for talking to me, Travis. I just needed a little bit of reassurance. I was really getting down on myself. I felt like the bad person in all this." Lefty said.

"Anytime, bub, anytime," Travis replied as he returned to a sleeping position on the couch.

"I'll see you Friday, Trav," Lefty said as he walked out the door.

CHAPTER 8

The next morning, Jim woke up to someone banging on his door. Jim slowly rose out of bed, put on a shirt, and house shoes. As he walked toward the front door, he squinted his eyes to try to see who it was. It was a sheriff's deputy. Jim opened the door and stood in the doorway.

"Hello, what's going on?" Jim asked the deputy. "Mr. Blakely, I'm sorry to have to wake you up. But the sheriff asked me to track down a man named Edward Whitehorse. Do you know where he is?" The deputy asked. "He will probably be working at the casino today," Jim replied. "Is that where he works?" The deputy asked. "Yeah. Oh, and everyone calls him Lefty. That's his nickname." Jim answered. "Ok, that helps me a lot, I won't keep you. Have a good day." The deputy said as he turned to walk toward his vehicle. Jim didn't think anything about it at the time. He assumed they wanted to ask Lefty routine questions and didn't give it a second thought. The longer he thought about it, the more worried he was. He thought that he needed to talk to Lefty and suggest that he get an attorney, if for no other reason than it is better to be safe than sorry. Jim picked up his cell phone and dialed Lefty. No answer. He then dialed Travis.

"I'm working, what the hell do you want?" Travis said as he was laughing. Jim could hear an auctioneer in the background, and that meant that Travis was at a cattle auction somewhere. "A sheriff deputy came by just a few minutes ago looking for Lefty. You think we need to make sure that Lefty hires an attorney? I don't think Lefty will want to, but I think he needs to." Jim said and waited for a reply. "It damn sure wouldn't hurt. Call your guy. If Lefty doesn't have the money, I'll split it with you if we have to loan him some money." Travis replied. "I'll call you as soon as I get out of here," Travis said and then hung up. Jim called his attorney, Mike Prescott. "This is Mike." A voice said. "Mike, this is

Jim. A sheriff's deputy came by looking for Lefty. I assume they want to question him. I think he needs an attorney. He is working at the casino today, and I haven't been able to get a hold of him." Jim said. "Keep calling Lefty, and when you get him, tell him to come to my office. I think I should be there when they question him just to be safe." Mike replied. "Ok, sounds good. Thank you, Mike." Jim said, then hung up. Shortly after Jim hung up with Mike, his phone rang again.

"Hello," Jim answered.

"The fruits of my labors manifested early today, so I'm fixing to get loaded and head out. Did you get a hold of your lawyer?" Travis expunged forth as eloquently as ever.

"Yes, he told me to try to get a hold of Lefty and have him go to Mike's office," Jim explained.

"Don't think that will happen. In Lefty's mind, he will be able to sit there in silence like a good, strong Comanche and intimidate his way out of this. As you know, I've sat in a jail cell alongside Lefty before when we got into that slight misunderstanding up in Tulsa." Travis said. Travis knew Lefty best, and Jim was well aware of that. Travis, on the other hand, also knew that Lefty would shoot himself in the foot a million times over just to save his pride. Travis thought and thought.

"Let's take Mike to Lefty," Travis suggested.

"I don't think Mike will do that. He stays pretty busy." Jim retorted.

"He's a god damned Lawyer! He would eat dog food, dress as a woman, and then sing about it on the morning news if you paid him enough!" Travis shot back. The idea of having an officer of the court ride around in his truck did not sit well with Jim.

"That won't hold water now that I think about it. Let's just see if we can find Lefty first before we add a damn lawyer to our traveling circus." Jim suggested. He continued, "What time will you be back in town?"

"Oh, by the time I get loaded and deliver this bunch of pasture pussy and get back, it will be about 3 o'clock," Travis answered. Jim was slightly taken aback and surprised by how Travis could come up with zingers constantly. He couldn't contain a giggle.

"Ok then. Pick me up at the store when you get back, and we will try to track down a Comanche." Jim said.

"Ok then, Captain Call," Travis said, then hung up.

Jim sat there in the serene darkness of his living room. He knew that today would be a complete shit show as in the Academy Awards of shit shows. It would be a multi-nominated, and multi-winner of all the shit shows that had ever been since Adam ate the apple just to get a little pussy. He chuckled to himself. He said out loud to himself that if he were Adam, God would have had to put a mature content warning in the atmosphere. Even when he was trying to cheer himself up, his mind shot back to the seriousness of the matter at hand. He knew that Lefty would not want to go to the attorney's office. He knew that trying to get Lefty to go to the attorney's office would be like trying to stuff a live deer in your truck. He finally pulled himself up, showered and shaved, and headed to get the shit show started.

Travis had delivered the load of "pasture pussy" as he called it, to his client. The client was very happy with the cattle Travis had acquired for him and paid Travis in cash, which put an extra pep in Travis's already natural, cheery disposition. As he drove down the highway on his way back to Bellville, Travis noticed flashing lights come on behind him shortly after he crossed the county line back into Haskell County. He had momentarily forgotten about his conversation with Jim until the flashing lights injected the memory back into him like a hot lead enema.

"Fuck me. This is going to be fun." He told himself, and he slowed and pulled over to the side of the road. As Travis put his truck in park, he looked at the patrol car in his side view mirror. The deputy made a grand display of putting on his sunglasses and an even gaudier gesture of putting his flat-brimmed hat on.

"God Damn!" Travis said to himself, laughing at the cop's gesture. The cop appeared to be no taller than five feet six or five feet six and a half at the most. As the deputy strutted toward Travis's truck, Travis started laughing so hard he spat his coffee. When the deputy got to Travis's driver's side window, he jerked his sunglasses off like Fabio in a butter commercial. "An insecure little man hasn't put on a show like that since Napoleon was scaring the hell out of Europe." Travis giggled.

"I don't listen to those communist European bands, sir!" The deputy replied in a raised voice.

Travis's laugh got louder at that comment.

"Do you know why I'm pulling you over, sir?" The deputy asked.

"No, sir, I do not," Travis replied.

"We're looking for that damn friend of yours, the one ya'll call Lefty." The deputy explained

"Where is he? Tell me now!" The deputy demanded.

"Ok, ok. Let me get out and give me about ten feet of room so I can pull a full-blood Comanche out of my ass!" Travis shot back.

"Don't mouth me, you son of a bitch! I know you know where he is, and I know you are hiding him!" The deputy yelled back.

Jim told the deputy that he did not know where Lefty was. After Travis got tired of this man with little man syndrome yelling in his ear, he said, "Hell, I'll call him right now and put him on speaker phone to prove it to you." Jim then picked up his flip phone and dialed Lefty on speaker phone. It did not ring and went straight to voicemail. After hearing Lefty's voice, the cop exhales slowly. At that point, the cop conceded defeat and gave Travis the standard order to contact law enforcement if he heard from Lefty. Travis just smiled and said thank you, then continued on his way.

Jim had done everything he could think of while he was at his store in Bellville. He reconciled the bank, finished up last month's financial statements, and even made a new daily shift checkout sheet to make the register closing process more precise. Stella had cried like a twelve-year-old girl who was left outside of a Justin Bieber concert when Jim showed her the new check-out sheet. Jim even did inventory, and still after all that still had an hour to kill before he could expect Travis to be there. Jim was anxious, and no matter how much he tried to keep his mind occupied, he worried about Lefty as if his own brother were missing. Lefty wasn't even missing, and Jim was still a nervous wreck on the inside. Jim went back to his office after failing in his search to find something else to do. He walked to his office chair, turned around, sat on his desk, and looked out the window directly behind his desk. As he saw the blue wooded mountains, his mind drifted to the camping trip and the fun he was having before hell broke loose. The whole trip replayed in his mind. Jim was totally absorbed in his own head. As he was lost in thought, Stella, one of his shift managers, said, "Jim! Jim!" Her words received no reply. Jim was still lost in his own little world of trance-like thoughts. Stella tiptoed forward a couple of steps to the edge of Jim's desk and picked up a stack of two large books on Jim's desk, held them aloft about a foot above the desk, and dropped them. A large echoing "Whack!" rang loudly throughout the office.

"Gaaaaaahhh!!!!, God Damn you! I almost fuckin' shit myself. Do you hear me?! I almost shit myself!" Jim said as his voice slowly decreased in volume as his reply ended.

Stella, by this time, was on her back, holding herself and laughing so hard she sounded like retarded turkey trying to talk. By the time she regained her composure, Jim's blood pressure had come back down to normal, and the pair could once again converse normally.

"I came to tell you that Travis is outside," Stella said, still trying to contain her laughter.

Jim said to her as he walked past her out of the office, "You may have to call a cleaning crew because I may have shit all over my desk!" That comment heralded the return of retarded turkey noises throughout the building as Stella began to laugh hysterically again. Jim walked out of the front doors and saw Travis's truck. Jim opened the passenger door and climbed inside.

Travis recounted the story of getting pulled over by Jim. Jim started giggling and said,

"I bet that cop is going to follow you around and look for an excuse to write your ass up for something."

"Probably. Now, where are we going to start to find Lefty?" Travis said as he got uncharacteristically serious.

"Let's start at the casino. He's got to be there or at home, and the casino is closer, so step on it, driver!" Jim responded as Travis backed out of the parking spot and drove toward the casino.

Lefty had clocked out, changed back into normal clothes from his security guard uniform, and was walking out the door into the parking lot when he noticed Travis's gray Ford pulling in. Lefty stood still and followed the truck with his eyes. No thoughts, no expression, just simply taking in all information he could before he responded in any way to the unusual sight of Travis or Jim coming to the casino, much less both tightwads at once.

Travis noticed Lefty. "There stands Lefty. He's standing still as a statue. He's probably wondering why in the hell both of us are showing up at the same time." Travis expunged.

"I'm tight as hell, but if it costs a nickel to shit, you would throw up!" Jim prodded.

"Yep. Especially if I have the opportunity to save the nickel and not waste toilet paper!" Travis said laughingly

Travis pulled up directly to where Lefty was standing. When Travis stopped the car, Lefty was standing directly beside Jim's passenger side window.

"Cops are looking for you." Travis blurted out.

"Thanks for being subtle there, pale face." Lefty shot back.

"You need to get in with us and get talk to Mike, my attorney. We already got you and an attorney because you will need one, whether you will admit it or not. Now get in, let's go," Jim demanded.

"I didn't do anything wrong. Why do I have to start acting like a criminal?" Lefty asked as his face descended into a look of confusion and fear.

"We know you didn't do anything wrong, but you know these trigger-happy hobbits that the sheriff has working for him now. One of their brethren carries a ring all the way to Mt. Doom, and they all think that we, normal-sized humans, should bow down. They don't care who is right and wrong; they want to turn on the big siren and use the big boy handcuffs once in their career." Travis replied, filling the air with his normal way of adding gobs of unnecessary words that left the recipient wondering when he would get to the god damned point.

"I don't have the money," Lefty replied calmly.

"We do, get in." Jim retorted.

Lefty looked back at the casino and then around the parking lot as if to try to see if anyone was witnessing their conversation. He slowly got in the back seat as Jim held the door open for him.

"You know I don't like any of this! A big part of me wants to head up to the mountains and shoot any idiot who tries to find me." Lefty said, showing a very rare sign of anger.

"Left, I wouldn't use that specific grouping of words when you're talking to Mike or the police. They don't appreciate fine oral eloquence the way you and I do." Travis suggested.

"Fuck you Honky. Now, drive Ms. Daisy to the law office," Lefty said in a high-pitched voice. The sheer shock of hearing Lefty make an attempt at humor left Travis speechless for the first time in the last few years.

CHAPTER 9

As the trio sat in the small lobby of Mike Prescott's office, silence reigned over the entire room. Mike's voice could be heard faintly coming from his office, which was in the next room on the other side of the wall that Travis, Jim, and Lefty had their back to.

"Mr. Blakely, you and your friends can go on in." The receptionist relayed in a kind voice. The sound of the kind voice soothed Jim's nerves for only a couple of seconds. Kind voices always have a way of fooling our minds. The effect of a kind, nice voice has a way of convincing our brains that everything will be ok, even if the slight serenity lasts only for a moment. The three roses from their chairs like some doomed trio on the way to a firing line. They walked the short distance into Mike's office. Mike was standing behind his large walnut stain colored desk. He reached his hand out to Jim. "Hey Jim, how are you doing?"

Jim tried to force a smile and was about halfway successful. "I'm hanging in there." He replied.

"Please have a seat. Let's go over where things sit." Mike said as he picked up a yellow legal pad and a pen. The three sat down like children who were in trouble, setting down to receive punishment from a father who was reluctant to punish his favorite children. Travis had gone nearly 10 minutes at this point without uttering a word. It was more than he could bear at this point, and he poured out his thoughts for the small captive audience. "Mike, do you need us to start talking, or is there some information you have that may cause a significant drop in our collective blood pressure?" Travis inquired in is usual style.

"I've got a couple of updates since I spoke to Jim. First, I wasn't able to talk to the D.A, but I was able to speak with the ADA. The deal is this: the cops and the DA think that Lefty should be questioned, then you,

Jim, then Travis. All separately. They want to use those statements to make a decision on whether to charge Lefty or not. They said they haven't even thought about what the charge would be and won't until the questioning is done. I don't think we should just let all that happen willingly. I think you three should each give written depositions, and we will submit those to the DA and the police. That way we can avoid any overzealous cops trying to make a name for themselves by being assholes and reading things into verbal statements that aren't there." Mike explained.

Nobody said anything for almost a minute. Jim finally spoke up. "OK, I think that's a good idea. We can keep Lefty away from the inside of a police station. Whether they admit it or not, they will treat him as if he just committed the Sharon Tate murders as soon as he walks in the door."

Mike nodded his head and replied with a simple "Yep." "Will they agree to written statements? And if they don't agree for some reason, will they accept the written statements? And why the hell can't they just go off of the police reports we gave at the time?" Travis asked.

"I apologize, guys. I don't mean another statement about what happened. What I meant was have them send their questions in writing, and we will send back a statement with answers in writing. Statement was a poor choice of words, and I apologize if I made you think you were going to have to give a whole other statement." Mike responded. Mike continued, "Edward, I'd like you to keep a few things in mind." Lefty didn't even seem to acknowledge that Mike was speaking to him. Lefty hadn't been called by his first name since his last doctor's appointment, which was over six months ago. Mike attempted a second time to get Lefty's attention. "Edward? Um, Mr. Whitehorse?"

Travis finally leaned over close to Lefty and spoke in a louder-than-normal voice. "Lefty! He's talking to you, Jackass!" Lefty jumped in his seat as Travis's smart-ass remark rang through his eardrums like an alarm clock in the silence of an early morning. "I'm sorry, Mike. I'm not used to being called by my real name." Lefty apologized as he was still trying to gather himself after Travis nearly scared him so bad that he almost reenacted the symptoms of cholera all over the chair that he was sitting in.

Mike looked at Lefty and started laying out his plan for what Lefty needed to do in the near term. "Ok, Mr. Whitehorse, I have talked to the police and the DA to make sure they know that an attorney represents you. They should know better than to try to come to your house and question you or come up to you at work and question you, etc. If they do try to question you, demand that you be allowed to contact me, and no matter what. I don't care if they ask you if the sun is hot or if the sky is blue! Do not answer anything unless I'm there with you." Mike explained to Lefty in a manner serious enough to get Lefty's attention. Both Travis and Jim were surprised that Lefty was being somewhat receptive to the advice and was seeming to cooperate willingly with what the attorney wanted him to do. "OK, I am usually pretty good at being quiet." Was Lefty's simple reply to Mike's orders. Mike stood up after that and said, "Well, that's all for now. Travis, Jim, do you want me to represent you also on this matter?" Mike asked. Jim and Travis, both told him yes since they both knew Mike, and they knew that Mike would look out for their interests and keep them pointed in the right direction. They were mainly worried about Lefty, and no amount of legal advice could change that worried feeling in their gut. As he walked to the truck, Jim was worried about Lefty, and he knew that if he was worried about Lefty, then Jim was for damn sure worried about Lefty.

As the trio of troubled wanderers rolled back into the casino parking lot to drop Lefty off at his own personal vehicular machine, Travis offered to buy Jim and Lefty dinner. Neither of them felt like dining out, so they politely declined. The three men went their separate ways for the evening. The next morning, Jim was found in his normal sedentary position on the side of his bed. The illumination beaming through his window had begun to play the role of a revered, un-answering oracle that Jim always found himself talking to every morning. Each morning, after he laid out the most pressing thoughts in his mind, he concluded that no answer was forthcoming and proceeded to the bathroom to shower and shave. Once Jim had made it out of the bedroom and past the dark green, melancholy-emitting walls of his living room, he was at the coffee machine, making coffee. A ringing sound was emitted from some unknown source. After a couple of seconds, it rang again. Jim suddenly realized that it was his cell phone. Jim rummaged around the drawer where he kept it. Jim always kept his phone in a kitchen drawer when he wasn't using it, mainly because he wanted no interruptions while he was doing non-cell phone things. He finally got the phone in his hand and answered it. "Hello," Jim said, unexcited about having to talk on the phone so early in the morning.

"Jim, they got him." The voice of Travis said. "They got who? And whose are they?" Jim replied

"Lefty, they arrested him. They drove out to his house this morning and arrested him!" Travis said as his voice kept getting louder and angrier as the sentence progressed. The information that Travis had told him hit like a baseball bat to the face. Jim held the phone away from his ear and stood there in stunned silence. All he could get his mind to focus on was the wind blowing through the trees outside his front door. Jim stood and watched the limbs sway in the wind, unable to muster a single coherent thought in response to the news. After a couple of minutes, shouts of "Jim! Jim! Jim!" could be heard from the cell phone. Jim slowly put the phone back up to his ear and said, "Um, I don't know what to say. This was a blindside. This is bullshit. I guess we need to let Mike know what's going on. How the hell did you find out, Trav?" Jim said after his brain finally got the gears moving to bring him back into focus. "I was his one phone call. I told him that I would go find you and go find Mike to see what we needed to do next." Jim explained. Jim thought for a couple of seconds about what the next step needed to be. "It's not even seven o'clock yet. Tell you what, meet me at Mike's office at 8. I doubt he will be there, but one of his secretaries will." Jim suggested a plan after being rendered into shock at the news of Lefty's arrest. "Damnit, Jim, you are one of the smartest people I know, but sometimes the dumbass creeps up on you from behind. You have a cell phone in your hand right now, and you have Mike's number. Call or text the son of a bitch." Travis said, pointing out the obvious that Jim did not see. "Yea, of course. I'll text him. Let's still plan on being at his office at 8. If anything changes after I talked to Mike, I'll text you." Jim explained, then hung up and began scrolling for the name "Mike Prescott" in his contact list.

CHAPTER 10

Travis sat in his truck in the parking lot of Prescott Law Office, PLLC. Travis had been reading the big black lettering on the gray brick wall ever since he pulled into the parking lot. He was scared, and when Lefty had called him from the jail, it was one of the few times in his entire life that he had been rendered speechless. After he had been sitting in the parking lot for what seemed like hours, he heard the sound of a vehicle pulling into the parking lot. It was Jim. Jim parked his truck next to Travis's, got out, opened the passenger door, and climbed inside Travis's truck. "What's the word?" Travis asked. "I got Mike on the phone. He said he had heard about Lefty's arrest shortly before I called him. He also said that the D.A. probably didn't tell him or any of us that Lefty was going to be arrested because he wanted it to be a surprise. Mike suspects that the D.A. was probably getting pressure to score a murder conviction or at least a murder arrest because of his reputation for doing nothing but cutting plea deals. Mike's going to meet us here. Should be here anytime." Jim explained. Jim and Travis sat in silence until 10 minutes had gone by, and Mike Prescott opened the front door of his office, stepped out of the door, and waved for Travis and Jim to come inside.

Jim's heart was pounding as he walked into the building and into Mike's office. Travis and Jim sat down in the chairs in front of Mike's desk. Mike sat down in his big office chair and pulled out a legal pad from a desk drawer. He pulled a pen from his shirt pocket and looked at Jim and Travis and said, "Ok, boys, this is where the game starts. The D.A has charged him with second-degree murder. Lefty is in the county jail; he will stay there until there is a bail hearing. The hearing is going to be today at 2 p.m. The D.A. has been fighting off a reputation of being a pussy, so he will fight like hell to get bail denied. I think that the judge will grant bail, somewhere in the neighborhood of five hundred thousand dollars." Mike explained.

"Hell, Lefty's place is paid for, isn't it?" Jim asked as he turned toward Travis.

Travis nodded. "Could he put up his place as collateral if bail is granted?" Travis asked Mike.

"I've already spoken with the bail bondsman that I recommend to clients, and he is fine with that. I did some quick research on Lefty's finances before I came to the office this morning." Mike said as he continued, "Both of you need to go about your normal lives. Don't talk to any reporters or anything. If you have a question about what to do, call me on my cell." Mike stood up as he finished explaining things to Jim and Travis. Jim knew that was the signal for him and Travis to leave and let him do his job. They shook hands with Mike and left him to his work. Travis looked at Jim after they got back to the parking lot and said, "Bub, I don't know about this; it just sits wrong in my gut."

"I know. It feels like there is a storm brewing, and we can't do a damn thing but try to hold on." Jim said. "Are you going to the bail hearing? I think Lefty will damn sure like to see us there." Travis said as he looked off into the distance, as if to hide the fear on his face from Jim.

"Yea. Meet you up there about 1:45," Jim said as he began walking to his truck.

Later on, that day, Jim and Travis found themselves sitting in a row of seating directly behind the defense table in the Haskell County district courtroom. Neither Jim nor Travis had said a word to each other since they arrived. Jim patted Travis on the back and held the courtroom door open to let Travis into the courtroom. That had been the extent of communication between the two since that morning's meeting at the lawyer's office. The door to the judges' offices opened, and Mike and the assistant district attorney came out into the courtroom, followed by Judge George T. Mortenson. Mike went to the defense table and whispered, "Hello, guys." To Travis and Jim as he sat down. Shortly after Mike sat down, Deputy Napoleon brought Lefty in. Lefty had on the customary orange jumpsuit and had handcuffs on his hands and feet. The sight of Lefty shackled like a monster from a movie made Travis giggle a little. It seemed like an adult dressed up in a hilariously inappropriate Halloween costume. It was hard for Jim to keep from smiling and laughing, especially when he saw Lefty in his new clothing and chains. Lefty turned the corner past the prosecution table and then walked over to the defense table. He looked over at Jim and Travis and raised his hands a little and whispered, "They think we are still the lords of the plains, I guess." Travis giggled again at the comment. It reminded Travis and Jim both why the three of them were best friends. Even in one of the direst situations a person could be in, they still found humor in the situation they were in. It was one of those moments that brought unexpected comfort for Lefty. It solidified in his heart that those two white boys would be with him until the end. If he asked them to give up everything, they would help him, without hesitating for a moment. Seeing his two best and only friends he trusted there for him, showing support for him during this scary moment, in front of a courtroom full of the fine people of Bellville, made Lefty feel as if an army of the great Numunu of the plains were behind him and ready to go to battle to defend their brother. Travis and Lefty obviously were not Comanche, and neither was anything close to a warrior, but in that moment, Lefty couldn't tell the difference.

While waiting for the judge to finish shuffling through a few papers that he had in front of him, Lefty turned toward Deputy Napoleon and asked, "Can you take the cuffs off of my feet? I'm not used to them, and I almost trip when I try to stand." The minuscule mass of anger and little man syndrome looked back at Lefty and snapped, "Nope! You're nothing but a danger to the people here, not taking them off." Travis scoffed at that remark and said louder than he intended, "Damn, Left, they think you're going to try to finish off adobe walls right here by yourself." The judge heard Travis's remark and laughed a little. "Uncuff his feet, deputy. He'll be fine." "Yes, uh, yes, sir." The deputy replied and uncuffed Lefty's feet. The judge ceased his paper shuffling and started to speak. "Edward Whitehorse, you have been charged with murder in the second degree. This charge is a very serious one. How do you plead?"

"Not guilty," Lefty said. "Ok, now comes the question of bail. What is the prosecution requesting?" The judge asked the assistant D.A.

"The prosecution requests that the defendant be remanded into custody. He is a security guard and a part-time hunting guide and could use the knowledge and skill to disappear or flee." Judge Mortenson cut him off. "Spare me the theatrical verbiage, counselor. I get the point." The judge said, and he pointed to Mike to signal him that his turn had arrived. "The defendant is an upstanding citizen, and though he does possess the skills mentioned by the prosecution, Mr. Whitehorse is dedicated to clearing his name and proving that he is absolutely innocent of this crime." Mike ended his pitch as the judge held up his hand. "I have reviewed Mr. Whitehorse's record, and it is clean. He has been nothing but cooperative with law enforcement. This is not a case of cold-blooded murder. The prosecution's evidence is shaky at best. Bail is hereby granted in the amount of one hundred thousand dollars." The judge declared as he wrapped his gavel. All parties stood up and began to gather their things and leave. "Split it with you, Jim," Travis said as he patted Jim on the back. "You got it," Jim replied. Mike shook Lefty's hand, said a few words, then turned to Jim and Travis.

"That went really well. I'll call my bail bonds guy straight away, so ya'll can go pick him up at the jail." Mike said. "Mike, Jim, and I are going to pay the bail for him. We will run over to the bank and get a cashier's check straight away." Travis said as he shook Mike's hand. "Ok, that will work fine. Take it to the court clerk, then he can get the hell out of jail." Mike said as he shook Jim's hand, then walked toward the door.

After sorting through the process of bailing out a prisoner, Travis and Jim went to the county jail to pick up Lefty. The pair exited Travis's truck and began walking to the front door of the jail when the notoriously confrontational deputy exited the building. "Well, look who it is. Do we see you about picking up our friend?" Travis asked the shorter man. "No, go see the person at the front desk." The deputy replied as he kept walking, with nothing more than a passing glance added to his reply. "I don't want to go in there, Trav. For some reason, that little bastard worries me. I'm going to stay out here and keep an eye on him." Jim told Travis as he found a bench in front of the building and sat down. "Alright, I'll be back as soon as I get him," Travis said as he continued walking to the front door. Jim sat down on the bench and looked out at the parking lot. The small deputy was rummaging through a pickup with sheriff department logos emblazoned all over it. Travis watched the deputy as he concluded his rummaging and walked to the bed of the truck, and appeared to attempt to retrieve something from the bed of the truck. Jim smiled and laughed quietly when he realized the deputy couldn't reach whatever he was trying to grab. "You need a step stool there, biggin?" Jim hollered. The deputy looked at Jim and shook his head, obviously pissed off at Jim's comment. It's usually Travis that spouts forth witty, smart-ass remarks, but Jim enjoyed his turn at it. Jim's phone vibrated in his pocket. He retrieved the phone and looked at the caller ID. It was Stella who was working that afternoon. "What's up?" Jim answered. "Nothing much, boss; everything is good here. I wanted to check on you." Stella explained. "I'm fine. Lefty got granted bail, and Travis is inside the jail now to get Lefty," Jim replied. "Ok, that's good news, Jim. Makes me feel better. If you need anything, Jim, I'm just a call away." Stella said in a tone that Jim noticed was a little more "friendly" sounding than normal. "Ok, appreciate it," Jim said, then hung up.

Travis heard the doors to the jail open and turned to see Lefty come out, followed by Travis. Jim stood and walked toward Lefty. Lefty gave Jim a hug, and Jim could see relief in Lefty's eyes. "Thank you for everything. I was just scared shitless ever since they first put me in the cell." Lefty said as they started walking toward Travis's truck. "Well, you're out now. What do you need first? Good food, or do you need to rest in a good bed?" Travis asked. "I just want to eat something and then go to bed. Travis, Mike called me right before I was released, and said that it may be a good idea to stay at your house tonight. He said the family of the people who tried to rob us are crazy hillbillies and may be incensed that I got bail." Lefty explained. "You're staying with me, chief," Travis said without any hesitation. Good friends who always did whatever they needed to help him made Lefty feel like he had a family. He already thought of Jim and Travis as brothers, but in times when they did everything that a biological brother would do, it made him feel as if they had been best friends for all of their lives. The mental weight and anxiety of killing someone still sat firmly on Lefty's shoulders, and the weight of that drug weighed down Lefty's emotions. But now, He had two others willing to help him carry that weight and fight right alongside him. Lefty resolved to fight on.

CHAPTER 11

The next morning Lefty woke up in Travis's spare bedroom on a futon. It was not exactly a traditional futon but rather a makeshift futon that Travis had built himself. Being a squeaky-tight bastard, Travis had no qualms about utilizing self-manufactured items to fulfill his needs even if they looked like a group of toddlers had built them. Lefty got dressed and put on his shoes and walked into the hallway. He could hear bacon sizzling in the pan. He could hear birds chirping outside. It was the sound of normal life, and Lefty breathed it all in like a liniment that soothed his mind. Lefty migrated toward the kitchen. The house had no separate dining room, just a dining area next to the kitchen. Lefty sat down at the end of the table facing out of the French doors that led to the backyard. "Morning, hope you're ready to eat," Travis said as he got two plates from the cabinet and sat them beside the stove. "Dig in, or else I will eat it all, cuz I'm gangsta like that." Travis quipped. Lefty burst out laughing. "I'm numunu, and I'm supposed to be strong, but you can spit out a few words and make me laugh like I have smoked weed all day." Lefty said as he rose to his feet and walked over to the stove. Travis fixed his plate, then walked over and sat on the side of the table in the chair closest to Lefty's chair. Lefty followed suit and sat down shortly after. "Damn, I can start anything without having to stop and piss. It's hell getting old." Travis complained as he rose and headed to the bathroom. Lefty noticed Travis had a small plate of biscuits and gravy next to his regular plate of bacon and eggs. Lefty reached over and grabbed the plate and started eating them. They tasted surprisingly good, and Lefty was savoring every bite. Travis returned to his seat and grabbed his fork. "Hey, you stole my damn biscuits and gravy!" Travis objected.

"I didn't steal it. I discovered it." Lefty replied without looking up.

After breakfast had concluded and Travis had performed a task that somewhat resembled doing the dishes, Lefty rose from the table and walked to the French doors at the back of the house and stared out at the backyard and beyond. What his eyes saw didn't matter to Lefty; he was looking past the scenery and letting his mind wander into what the future may hold. Inside he was terrified of the prospect of a murder trial that loomed over his and his friend's heads. A part of his soul felt ashamed. Ashamed of the situation he was in, ashamed that his best friends were caught up in this mess with him. The voice of Travis broke Lefty's trance. "What the hell are we going to do today?" Travis asked. Travis didn't wait for Lefty's reply; he just replied for him by saying, "You are going to ride around with me today and visit some of the esteemed clients of Livingston Agricultural Consulting, Inc." He declared while he put his wallet and cell phone in his pockets. "I don't work again until Tuesday, so today, Sunday, and Monday I should probably lay low, or at least that's what Mike suggested. I'm supposed to meet with him Monday afternoon." Lefty said as he began to gather his own wallet and cell phone and began the search for footwear. "Good, he'll just ride around with me. Hell, let's get a 12-pack. We will steal one of Jim's employees to drive us around if we get drunk." Travis said as he began walking toward the door. "You do that?" Lefty replied, somewhat taken aback at the comment. "Hell yeah, it ain't free though. That squeaky bastard will bill me for it, but it's cheaper than a DUI, and I deduct the labor on my tax return, so instead of calling her a designated driver, I call her a walking tax shelter." Travis said, his logic making him giggle. "Pale face still fucking the system." Lefty replied as the pair got into Travis's truck, laughing and smiling. Lefty was thankful to know the feeling of laughter again.

While Lefty and Travis were planning a day of laying low and violating the transportation of open container laws, Jim was in his office at his Belleville store. It was only 9:30 am, and he had already worked to a standstill. He had nothing really left to do. He had worked up the daily deposit from the previous day's sales, he had triple-checked each cashier's new checkout sheet that Jim was so proud of, and he had lent a hand sweeping and cleaning the windows. Now, Jim sat at his desk and was watching Netflix on his computer. Jim was watching Trailer

Park Boys, and it had brought several large smiles to his face, but no laughter. The worry on his mind was like a large stone wall preventing laughter from penetrating his soul. Stella came into his office and sat on the end of his desk and leaned over to see what was on Jim's computer screen. "What the hell are you watching? I could hear someone yell the word "cocksucker" down the hall." She said as she smiled with a mixture of curiosity and laughter on her face. "That was Bubbles. He is the brains of the trailer park and the coolest son of a bitch that ever lived." Jim responded without taking his eyes off the screen. "Can I watch with you?" Stella said as she got up from the edge of his desk and walked around to Jim's side of the desk. "Don't you have work to do? It's not even ten o'clock yet?" Jim replied, looking up from the screen and eyeing her suspiciously. "I had a handsome older man helping me clean this morning!" She shot back with a bubbly smile. "Oh yea, I am rather good-looking. I take my good looks for granted sometimes. I apologize." Jim retorted as he reclined his chair and returned his gaze to Ricky, Julian, and Bubbles on his screen. Stella laughed and pointed when she laid eyes upon bubbles for the first time. "Hahahaha, that is fucking golden!" She laughed and pointed at the screen. When she lowered her hand, she rested it on Jim's shoulder as she continued to stand behind Jim's office chair. Jim glanced at the hand but didn't brush it away. He refrained from brushing Stella's hand away, but he couldn't determine why. Jim didn't want anything else to worry about, that was for damn sure, but wasn't up for whatever would become of him brushing away what could potentially be a totally innocent gesture. "Yeap, it's the best. Even better when you're drunk." He replied. Stella's hand moved across his chest into almost a full hugging motion. Stella reached down and kissed Jim on the cheek and uttered, "See you later, got to manage this empire." And left the office and headed back out into the store area. "Shit. Somehow, someway, this will come back to give me a strong dose of pain in my posterior." Jim told himself as he focused back on his TV show.

Jim got tired of watching TV after a couple of episodes and grabbed his deposit with the full intention of taking it to the bank. As he walked out of his office and down the hall to the store area, he could hear the song "Shin Kicker" by Rory Gallagher playing so loud he could almost feel the sound waves as he walked up to the front door to see what was going on. Jim was a big fan of Rory Gallagher, so he recognized the song instantly. He saw Travis's truck in a parking spot. The truck's engine was running, but there was no sign of Travis. Jim then turned toward the cash register counter and saw Rashad. Rashad pointed toward the bathroom and said, "Travis and Lefty just went into the bathroom. Which makes me nervous because they appear to have consumed alcohol." At first, Jim walked and stood by the counter to wait for his two compadres to emerge from the restroom. Then he looked toward Travis's truck. An idea manifested in Jim's brain. Jim slid his deposit into his back pocket and walked out the front door to Travis's truck. He tried to open the driver's side door, and it was open. He got in and put the truck in reverse and backed out of the parking spot. Jim then drove the truck to the south side of the building, out of view of anyone who was in the store area. Jim locked the truck and stuck the keys in his pocket. He returned inside shortly before he could hear the door to the bathroom open and hear Travis's voice singing out of key, "Well, it's a shin-kicking morning; gotta kickstart the day!" Jim stood still and watched Travis as he walked toward the hallway that led to Jim's office. As he walked past the front door and peered out into the parking lot. Travis came to a full stop and looked back at the cashier. Travis then walked out of the front door and could be heard saying, "Well, goddamnit!" Travis walked back in the store and saw Jim standing by the counter. "Just my fucking luck, bud. Pay the motherfucker off, and it grows legs. Fuck me running!" Jim said as he put his hands on his hips and stomped his feet. Lefty walked up to the cashier with a bag of chips and a bottle of water. Lefty laughed and glanced toward Travis. "I now know how to sober up a cowboy quickly. Steal his truck." Lefty said as he laughed a low-sounding laugh that came from deep down. Lefty had to put a hand on the counter and put a hand on his belly due to the pain of laughing so hard. "Well fuck a duck and call it a shishkabob!" Travis said, leaning against the counter beside Jim. Travis looked at Jim with a look of pissed-off confusion and extreme chagrin. Jim lost it and busted out laughing. The kind of laugh where the sheer force of the laugh made you throw your head back and let it all out. "This ain't that fucking funny!" Travis said, raising his voice to a lever that indicated that his blood pressure was behaving similarly. Jim kept on laughing as he reached into his pocket and gave Travis back his keys. Travis immediately punched the lock button on the key fob twice and heard the honk of his truck. "Fuck you! I guess you're going to sell this place and go on the road with that act, since you're so goddamn funny." Travis said with a small smile starting to grow. "What are ya'll doing anyway?" Jim asked. "Lefty and I have been riding around drinking beer. Needed to relax and try to ward off some of this stress." Travis explained. "Cool. Ya'll are wanting a DD, aren't you?" Jim replied.

"Yep!" Travis quipped. "Alright." Jim agreed and hollered at Stella. "Stella! You got all your stuff done?" "Yea, all done unless it gets really busy." She replied. "You want to make some extra money being me, Lefty, and Jim's DD for a couple of hours?" He asked. "Yea! Let's go!" Stella answered as she held her hand out to Travis in a gesture to ask for his keys. Lefty, Travis, and Jim followed Stella out the door.

CHAPTER 12

After loading up on beer, Travis, Lefty, and Jim rode to the bank so that Jim could make the deposit he had completed this morning. Stella was driving with Mariah Carey turned up loud on the radio. One of Stella's rules for when she was the designated driver was that she got to pick all the music. The song "Fantasy" was blaring on the radio with Stella singing at the top of her lungs when the group of nomadic semi-alcoholics rolled into the bank drive-through. Stella was kind enough to turn the volume down enough to allow Jim to hear the teller. Jim was in the front seat and handed the deposit to Stella, who in turn put the deposit in the drawer. The teller retracted the drawer and began working on the deposit. The clacking of buttons and murmuring of tellers could be heard, indicating that the microphone system that allowed the tellers to hear the customers was still on. Travis and Lefty giggled about something. Travis leaned up to the front seat and said rather loudly, "Ask them if they got any ice!" Jim turned and looked at Travis. "This is the damn bank drive-through, not the Git-n-Go! They don't have any damn ice for us! We already got plenty of ice!" Jim responded, still experiencing a slight amount of shock at Travis's request. Lefty leaned back in his seat. This, he thought, was exactly what he needed. Low-key entertainment to take some of the enormous stress off of him, if only for a small amount of time. Half an hour later they were on a dirt road with no trouble in sight. Travis was singing Rory Gallagher songs loudly, while Stella had Lady Gaga playing. Jim couldn't help laughing. Lefty didn't say much; he just did a lot of laughing and smiling. Which Jim was glad to see. The backroading adventure began to wind down when Jim and Travis realized they needed a nap. They arrived back at Jim's store, and they all proceeded to the bathroom to empty their bladders for what seemed like the 100th time. After Jim emerged from the restroom, he ordered Rashad and Stella to drive

Travis and Jim to their respective houses and then return to the store. Stella instructed Rashad to drive her car and follow her and to pick her up once they dropped Travis off. Jim manned the cash register in their absence and had to give it the old college try to stay awake.

Half an hour later Rashad and Stella walked through the front door, their task complete. Jim left his post and began walking to his office without a word. He needed a nap. Jim sank into his office chair, put his feet up, and let his world fade to black. Sometime later, Jim was awakened by Stella shaking his shoulder. "Jim, the shift is over. The evening shift is fixing to take over. Do you need a ride? Come on, I'll drive you." She said. Jim protested and informed her that he was perfectly fine. His opinion was altered when he experienced dizziness when he stood. He agreed to let Stella drive him home. Jim left his office and walked outside to his truck. To his surprise, Stella didn't get anyone to follow her. Jim was too tired to worry about it and fell asleep as Stella backed out of the parking spot. When they arrived at Jim's house, it was almost five o'clock. Jim awoke as they pulled up in front of his house and pulled himself out of his truck. Stella found his house key on his key ring and opened the front door. Jim was still too tired to be alert enough to worry about what Stella was doing or how she was getting back to the store, so he kicked off his boots and trudged his way down the hall to his bedroom.

He fell back onto his bed and began to drift off to sleep. He heard his bedroom door close. He thought that Stella was shutting the door so that Jim could get some peace and quiet. To his surprise he heard footsteps inside his bedroom still. He felt someone crawl over him and get under the covers on the other side of the bed and heard Stella say, "Now, let's get some rest." Jim wanted to tell her no, but he was too tired and way too relaxed at that moment. Sometime in the evening, Stella had woken Jim to make her move, and Jim didn't protest at all. He let it happen, and he enjoyed it. Though Stella was 10 years younger than Jim, they had grown close since she began working for him. Jim had no clue this would ever happen, but he allowed himself to go with the flow. The next morning, the same beam of light began its morning vigil. Jim stopped in the natural spotlight and let the sunlight warm him for a moment. Once he got to the bathroom door, he turned back and looked at his bed. Stella was sprawled out asleep on his bed, her long dark hair covering her chest like an intricate tattoo. Jim shook his head and proceeded to the bathroom to shower and shave. When Jim emerged from the bathroom, freshly showered and shaved, he got dressed and proceeded to the kitchen to make himself some coffee. After a short war of patience against the coffee machine, he settled down on the couch with a fresh cup of coffee to relax.

Jim's cell phone rang. It was a muffled-sounding ring that sounded like it was on the other side of the house. Jim rose from his state of relaxation to begin the search. As he walked down the hall that was dimly lit by the morning sunshine creeping through the windows, he could tell the ring was coming from his bedroom. Jim walked into the bedroom and determined that the ring was coming from his phone that was still in his pants pocket. Jim retrieved the phone and answered it. "Hello." His simple answer was. "Hey, what the hell are you doing this morning?" Travis asked.

Jim glanced toward the bed and noticed that Stella was not in the bed. He glanced toward the bathroom and saw that the bathroom door was closed, and the light was on inside. "Well, I just made some coffee and was relaxing on the couch. Some asshole decided to interrupt my serene morning by calling my phone." Jim replied. "Oh hell, serene my ass. What the hell else do you have to do besides talking to me?" Travis inquired. "The question is not what, but rather who." Jim responded. Halfway surprising himself. Jim knew it would get out sooner or later that Stella had spent the night with him. Stella had been texting her friends earlier that evening that she wasn't going to make their morning jog, so Jim figured some people had already put two and two together. "Wait a minute! Hold the phone! What?" Travis shot back surprised that his old friend had finally let his humanly impulses come back to life again after a long absence. "Yea, tell you about it later. What's up anyway? I know you didn't just call to chat." Jim pushed. "Yea, Mike called Lefty and wanted us to come to the office today to chat about something. He said it was important and that he wanted me and you to come." He explained. "Damn, it must be important if he is wanting to meet on a damn Sunday," Jim said as he began looking for his shoes. "Meet me and left there at 10:30. I think her son of a bitch is using us as an excuse to get out of church with his wife. Bye." Travis shot back and then hung up. A normal person would be taken aback at how abruptly Jim and his friends ended their conversations on the phone. Travis Jim and Lefty all did the same thing, and they each agreed that once the gist of the message had been delivered, there was no reason to continue on. Jim walked back into the bedroom to search for Stella. She was sitting up in bed scrolling on her phone. "Morning," he said. "Good morning, big sexy!" She shot back. Jim was slightly embarrassed at that remark. "Oh hell," he replied. He laid back onto the bed next to her. She put down her phone and rested her chin on his chest and looked at him face-to-face. She kissed him. "I'm not scheduled to work today. You want to hang out?" She asked. "What do you mean, hang out?" He asked slightly suspiciously. Jim was not in the mood to take Stella out on a date; he had too much on his mind. "Oh, I don't know. Like I'll hang out with you while you do whatever you do on Sunday!" She replied with an annoying level of cheer in her voice. "Well, I got to meet Lefty and Travis at the attorney's office at 10:30, and then I'm going to go check on the store over in Helens." Jim answered. "Ok, how about I just ride with you over to Helen's?" Stella said in a tone that hinted she was insisting on accompanying him. "Oh, hell alright. What do you want to do while I go to the attorney's office?" He asked. "Drop me off at the store, I'll get my car and go home and change, then you can pick me up after your meeting." Stella suggested. "Sounds like a plan. Let's go." Jim agreed. They got up and left the dark room, leaving the beam of light to search a soulless room.

After disposing of the slightly annoying ball of good cheer at the store, Jim arrived at Mike Prescott's office at 10:15. Travis's and Lefty's trucks were both there. Travis and Lefty were talking just outside the front door to the office. Jim got out of his truck and walked over to where Travis and Lefty were standing. He hit the lock button on his key fob twice to lock his truck. Jim's truck honked in confirmation that it was locked and secure. Lefty jumped a few inches off of the ground when Jim's truck honked. "Damn Indian! Little jumpy, are ya?" Jim said as he laughed.

"I thought ya'll weren't scared of white men?" Travis said not to pass up the opportunity to pile on during this rare showing of emotion by Lefty. "Only scared of them when they are behind me honking loud fucking horns!" Lefty said, finally letting a grin show. "That wasn't on purpose! If it was, I would be bragging." Jim said to Lefty. Lefty flipped him off as Travis held the door open for them. "Enter into thy kingdom of bullshit!" Travis said, waving a hand in dramatic fashion to beckon Lefty and Jim to enter. They all made their way into Mike's office, who was sitting at his desk making notes on a legal pad. "Good morning, gentlemen!" Mike said in a cheery voice. Jim was thinking to himself that every homo-sapiens with a hole in their ass was awful god damn cheery today.

They all sat down as Lefty said, "So, what's up? Anything change or something?"

"Yes, things have changed." Mike answered. "Fuck!" Lefty said as he leaned back into his chair.

"No, it's ok. Things have changed for the better." Mike shot back. He continued. "The D.A. doesn't have any corroborating witnesses and doesn't have any evidence to support the charges he's filed. His only witness is the guy that survived the robbery attempt. Matter of fact, his name is Wilkins, Robert Wilkins. Lefty, the person you shot was named James Wilkins. They both have a record a mile long. Not credible. I've spoken to the judge, and he strongly hinted that he doesn't believe any charges are appropriate in this matter. Let's file a motion to dismiss all charges due to lack of evidence. Now is the time to strike." Mike concluded his presentation. "Hell of an idea. Two questions I got. One, what are the chances it goes well, and two, what happens if we don't win the motion?" Travis asked as he sat up in his chair and looked directly at Mike. Jim turned his eyes from Travis to Mike, his interest in Mike's reply attracting his attention. "I think our chances are 80%. If we lose, then we go on to trial. More likely the D.A. would offer a plea at that point but were not taking a plea." He replied. "I like the idea. What about you Lefty?" Jim said as he looked at Lefty in anticipation of a reply. "Let's do it." Lefty replied. "Ok, then today is October 1st, so I will get it set for Wednesday, October 4th. They all agreed and shook hands. Jim, Lefty, and Travis said goodbye, agreed to eat dinner at Jim's house, and then all departed for their own winding paths toward evening ribeyes and Coors Light.

CHAPTER 13

After the meeting at Mike's office, Jim had picked up Stella, and they headed toward Jim's second store in Helens. Jim had a retired CPA named Jack Hendry who acted as a manager of the store. Jack had outlived his wife and had two sons who lived in New Mexico and Frankfurt, Kentucky, so he was in desperate need to find something to occupy his time. Jim had known Jack from the days when he worked at the accounting firm. The two worked together briefly and had attended some of the same continuing education conferences. Jack worked about 3 hours a day, implemented Jim's orders that Jim sent to him via email, and enjoyed his part-time managing gig. When Stella and Jim arrived at the store and walked into the front door, Jack had a cash register sideways and was messing with the back cord. "Hey Jim! How are you doing?" Jack said. "This damn power cord kept shorting out or something, so I sent Dana to run to Walmart and grab another one. Working good now." Jack explained. "Sounds good Jack, that's why you're the best!" Jim replied. "Hey Stella, beautiful as ever this morning!" Jack greeted Stella as he grabbed his coffee cup and walked out from behind the counter. "Everything going good, Jim. Need another person for the afternoon shift but, we will fill it quick." Jack reported. "Good deal. You got big plans this afternoon? Looks like you're all shined up!" Jim said, noticing Jack's pressed jeans and ironed shirt. "Nah, just a couple of friends of mine are going over to Fort Smith to a senior citizen's dance. "Pimpin'!" Stella smiled and said. "Hell, just something to do is all." Jack said, his face reddening slightly at the compliment from Stella. "Well, I'm off, Jim. See you next week if not sooner!" Jack said as he grabbed his jacket and left.

Jim had done his customary Sunday inspection of his store. He checked the shelves to make sure they were clean and had no out of date items, he checked so see make sure the floors were clean also. Jim had already swept the floors twice since he had arrived because it just convinced his mind that it was cleaner that way. He washed the outside of the building with a pressure washer, getting rid of some dirt and spider webs that had accumulated. Jack made the deposits for Jim, but Jim was still a stickler for making Jack take a picture of the count sheets and deposit calculation spreadsheets and send them to Jim every day. On Sunday Jim looked over everything from the week and prepared the deposit himself. Jim had no office, just a perch behind the counter where the customers couldn't see him but allowed enough room for him to work. After concluding all his work and becoming bored, Jim looked around for Stella. He found her consulting with the cashier about what color she should change her hair to. "You ready?" Jim asked as he took his keys out of his pocket. "Yeah! Let's go!" Stella shot back in the same annoying bubbly cheer. "See ya, Jamie!" she said to the cashier as she put her jacket on. Stella walked up to Jim and kissed him on the mouth. Jim was shocked that she did that out in the open, in front of other people. Stella had kissed him and kept walking as if it had been part of her routine for years. Jim didn't know how to respond. He just sighed and followed her out the door. On the drive back home, Jim had driven in silence. Stella was poking at her cell phone and giggling. "When they were pulling into Bellville," Jim asked. "Am I dropping you off at your house?" Jim asked. Jim, like most men, did not possess a mastery of the force that could allow them to know what the hell a woman was thinking. "Do you want me to drop you off?" Stella shot right back. "Shit," Jim said quietly to himself. "It's either that or the old Ford here is going to naturally head for home with you in it." Jim replied as he smiled at her. "Drop me at my house. If you want, I could drop by later." Stella suggested. "Ok." Jim said, keeping his eyes on the road. "You have to say it though!" Stella said. That comment caught Jim by surprise. "Say what?" He asked, slightly confused. "You have to say you want me to come by. I obviously like you, but you gotta like me too." Stella said. Jim thought for a minute or so and finally relented. "I want you to come by later." That comment caused a smile to manifest itself on her face. By that time, they were close to Stella's house. Jim pulled his truck into her driveway and put his truck in park. Now for the awkward part, the main thought going through his head as he put his truck in park. Stella took all the awkwardness out of the situation when she climbed over the center console and into Jim's lap. She kissed him, opened his driver-side door, and said, "See you later, old man." She strode down the sidewalk to her front door. Jim put his truck in reverse and backed out of the driveway. He saw her wave at him as he drove away.

Jim stopped by his Belleville store before going home. He needed some beer and bread. He pulled up to the front of the store. There were a few cars parked in front and a few people in the store. Normally Sunday afternoons were the slowest part of the week, so a few customers milling around was a good sign. Jim found his 12-pack of Coors Light and a loaf of bread and put them up on the counter. Jim always paid for his own items. He always wanted to set an example that he paid his own way just like his employees did. Even though it wasn't a big deal, the employees saw it, and it made them feel like he considered them an equal. Little things like this are why his employees enjoyed working for Jim. "Boss, we had a good day today; lots of people came in," the cashier told Jim as he scanned Jim's items. "What's your gross so far?" Jim asked. The cashier hit a few buttons on the POS system while Jim leaned over the counter to see. "Damn! That is good." Jim surprisingly showed up, and he spoke the words. He told the workers to keep up the good work and headed home. He wanted a nap before Stella showed up.

CHAPTER 14

Jim awoke to the sound of his cell phone ringing. He fumbled around the recliner and found his phone and answered it. "Hello!" he said. "Damn, did I wake your ass up?" Travis said. "Yep. Hell, I probably would have slept all the way until morning." Jim said. "Me and Lefty are on our way over. We saw some ribeyes on sale at Walmart, so we picked up a few." Travis explained. Jim shot bolt upright. He had forgotten that Travis and Lefty were coming over for dinner. He finally was able to overcome his initial panic and said, "Alright, I'll get the grill fired up. See you in a few." He had already told Stella that he wanted her to come over, but he had totally forgotten that Travis and Lefty were coming over for supper. Jim finally concluded that Travis and Lefty were going to find out about Stella eventually, so he decided to call Stella and tell her to come on over for supper. She dialed her number, and Stella answered on the first ring. "Goddamnit!" Jim said silently to himself. He was hoping for three or four rings to give him time to think of what to say. "Hey there," Stella said in her normal cheerful voice. "I'm cooking steaks. Come over and eat. Travis and Lefty are coming over too." Jim said, impressing himself that he didn't say anything stupid. "Oooh, you're going to let me meet your friends?" Stella said in a teasing voice. "Yep. It's happening." He shot back. "You know, after tonight more and more people will know about us." She said, "Are you ok with that?" She asked. "I'm fine with it if you are." He answered. "I am! Are you fixing to cook?" She asked. "Yeap, Travis and Lefty are on the way over." He said. "Ok, I'll head over that way." She said that and then hung up. Jim got out of his recliner and headed to fire up his grill. Jim was hoping like hell that Stella arrived before Travis and Lefty did. He did not want to have to explain why in the hell Stella was strolling into his house like she had been there a million times in front of those two. The hell he would catch would be damn near unbearable. Not only him, but Stella would catch her fair share of hell too. It would all be in good fun, of course, but if Stella was there first, Jim felt more comfortable introducing her right off the bat and getting the news of their newfound relationship the hell out of the way. As Jim was turning on the propane, he heard a car door shut, followed shortly by the front door opening. Once he had the grill lit and heating up, he walked in the house to see who it was. He entered the kitchen through his back door to find Stella putting a six-pack of Michelob Ultra in the fridge. "Getting ready to tie one on?" Jim asked as he walked into the kitchen. "Damn straight! I thought I may need a buzz to get through the hell we are both fixing to catch." She retorted. Jim was extremely relieved to know that Stella was expecting to catch hell; it would make it go over more smoothly. "Yeah, I don't think it will be too bad. With all that's gone on lately, I think they both will be ready to relax." Jim said. "You can wish in one hand and shit in the other." Stella laughed at his hopeless remark. "You're now." She paused as she looked toward the ceiling in thought. "What shall we call it? Fuck it, let's just call it what it is. You have been fucking an attractive younger woman, who happens to really like you as well." Stella declared as she put her arms around him and kissed him. "Now, cook me a ribeye, fucker." She slapped his ass and opened herself a beer.

Stella was out on the back porch standing at the grill, unable to resist the urge to go check on the steaks herself, when Travis and Lefty arrived. "The party has arrived! Get ready, bitches!!" Travis exclaimed in his usual ornate oratory. "Yes, let's yell it as if Jim doesn't see your loud ass twelve feet in front of him." Lefty added in as they saw Jim in the kitchen holding a beer. "Oh hell, kiss my ass. Now Jim, as consumed as my mind was inculcating the classy yet humorous announcement of our entry, I did notice that there is a little silver car in your driveway. Anything you want to tell us." Travis zapped all hopes of easing into the awkwardness Jim was hoping to postpone for at least a few minutes. Lefty was setting steaks on the counter as he looked out a back window and noticed Stella at the grill. "Jim, there is an attractive white woman at the grill. I'm guessing that solves the mystery of the little silver car." Lefty observed. "Yep, I and Stella have been fucking. And yes, I enjoy it." Jim admitted. "Welp, you just got right to it. Hell, I didn't even have to needle it out of you. You must like this girl." Travis shot back. "Yeah, I do." Jim cut his sentence short as Stella came in the back door and walked into the kitchen. "Hey guys!" Stella said in an upbeat voice. "Jim here has just informed us that ya'll have been fornicating, and I and Lefty wish to convey our congratulations." Travis said as he stepped over to give Stella a hug. "You're not going to give us nine kinds of hell?" Stella replied. Lefty went over to Stella and gave her a short hug and said, "We are pleased that someone turned his bedroom into an enjoyable place from the doom and gloom it has been for the past few years." "How are you holding up, Left?" Stella asked. "I'm doing ok. We had a good meeting with the attorney today, so I feel a little better." Lefty answered. "That's good; do you want a beer?" She asked. Lefty held up his Coors Light and said, "Step ahead of you!" Lefty smiled as they all migrated to the back patio and the grill. The steak cooking was accomplished without fail, and they all began to eat shortly after. After their bellies were full and Jim and Lefty had the dishes cleaned and into the dishwasher, Travis collected beer cans from the collection of empties in the trash can and walked to the fence at the edge of Jim's backyard. He placed the cans on the top row of the barbed wire fence by hanging them by the tab onto the barbs. There was an art to it, and Travis was the master of making it look easy. Travis returned to the back patio and said, "Stella, this is the kind of shit we do. Drink beer and shoot shit." Stella hopped to her feet and said, "Hell yeah!!" Jim went into the house and retrieved his lever-action Rossi 22 rifle. The contest consisted of betting each other on how many times out of 3 they could hit the target. The bets normally included one-hundred-dollar bills, the loser having to sing and dance for the rest of the group, and other comical ventures. Lefty was, by far, the most seasoned shooter among them; he rarely ever missed. Travis and Jim were pretty close to being tied for second-best shooter. Three rounds into the action, Lefty has displayed his normal brilliance with a firearm, and the others conceded defeat. "Have ya'll had enough? I'm just hitting my stride." Lefty announced. "I shot my best I have in a long time, and I still lost by two." Jim answered as beer bottles could be heard opening once again, and lawn chairs began to become occupied again.

"Well, tomorrow is Monday, the first part of the month again. Fuck Me." Travis said as he took a drink of his beer. "Yeah, don't remind me.

Every swinging dick will be in the store trying to buy beer and cigarettes with their EBT card." Jim complained. "All these damn Republicans want to bitch about food stamps, but none of them will enforce anything and stop the fraud in all the stores." Jim lamented further. "Hell no." Stella said as she stood up and continued. "Solving the problem will take away one of their talking points." She said, sympathizing with Jim's complaint. She went into the house in search of a place to relieve herself. "Damn, Jim, I never took you for a Democrat. Are you getting all soft and hippie-like in your advancing age?" Travis inquired after Stella went inside. "I'm not, still independent as they come, but damn, idiots are idiots, regardless of party." Jim explained as he lifted his beer to take a drink, satisfied with his condemnation of the current state of politics. While Stella was in the bathroom, Travis could not contain himself. He had to ask Jim about Stella. "So, bub, how did you land Stella?" He asked Jim. Jim thought for a moment, as if to feign deep thought. "Hell, I really don't know," Jim answered. "What I really want to know is are you playing the long game? Or is it a short-term physical thing?" Travis finally said, getting to the point. "Don't know yet, still just taking it easy, day by day. Not planning anything long-term yet." Jim answered. "Good. Because eventually she will leave your old ass for someone who can close down the electric cowboy with her." Lefty said, interjecting himself into the conversation. "You're probably right, Left. But in the meantime, I'm going to enjoy myself." Jim declared as Stella emerged from the house. "Did everything come out alright?" Jim asked. "Ain't no coming and going to happen until your friends leave." Stella shot back, eliciting a chorus of "oooohs" from Travis and Lefty. "Well, it's past ten. Which means it's about 45 minutes past my bedtime." Travis said as he rose and began to clean up his empties. "I'm ready to go home and sleep for the next 12 hours." Lefty said as he began to clean up after himself also. Once they had cleaned up after themselves and obtained Travis's fabled ice chest, they said their goodbyes and went on their way. That left Stella and Travis alone on Jim's back porch. Stella smiled at Jim, then reached out and ran her finger down Jim's cheek. "Are you happy, babe?" She asked Jim. "I am. I'll be happier when Lefty is out of the woods, though. You sure do make the days go by easier." He said as he sat pondering the backyard. When it was dark, the large light he had on the back of the house lit up the backyard like a rodeo arena. That's what first gave Jim and his friends the idea of shooting cans. Jim made the observation that it was bright enough to shoot at night. Lefty had jumped at the chance to show off his shooting skills. It had become an almost weekly tradition. Stella stood up and held out her hand, signaling to Jim that she wanted him to do the same. He grabbed her hand and stood up. "Bedtime." She said as she winked at him and led him inside. One thing Jim had learned about Stella was that when the urge hit her, she was ready, and she didn't care what room of the house they were in. In the current moment, they had barely made it to the living room when Stella had turned around and given him that look. She laid back onto the couch and instructed Jim to begin. He obliged.

CHAPTER 15

Monday morning found Jim and Stella on the couch. Once he awoke, Jim crawled out from under Stella, who had fallen asleep on top of Jim. He never seemed to need an alarm clock. Every morning around 6:30 am Jim woke up. This morning was no exception. He made his way to his bedroom, then into his bathroom for a shower and shave. He hadn't finished his shower when Stella joined him. They had their fun, and 30 minutes later they were on their way to town. "Drop me at my house; I don't work until eleven." Stella said. "Ok. I'll drop you off, and then I'm headed over to the store." Jim replied. "You want me to fix you lunch? I got leftover steak. I'm going to make myself a sandwich." Stella asked. "Nah, Travis and Lefty are meeting me at the Mexican joint. We will solve all the world's problems as well." Jim replied. A small look of disappointment passed over Stella's face after he turned her down for lunch. "Ok, so will I see you later?" She asked. "Yep." He replied as she leaned over to kiss him. She did her customary exit, climbing over Jim's lap and kissing him on her way out. He found his hat that had fallen off during Stella's exit, put it back on, and backed out of Stella's driveway. He felt somewhat relieved to be back by himself. It seemed like he hadn't had any alone time since Stella started spending time with him. He was ready to get Lefty's ordeal behind him and get his life back to normal. He arrived at his store, anxious to get started on the day.

Shortly after ten o'clock, the sheriff and the one who Travis referred to as Deputy Napoleon came into the store. Jim was back in his office reconciling a bank statement and heard their voices when they asked the cashier if Jim was available. When Jim heard them ask for him, he walked out front. "There he is!" The sheriff exclaimed as he saw Jim emerge from the hallway that led to his office. "What can I do for you, Sheriff?" Jim asked as he forced himself to shake the sheriff's hand.

"Need to talk to you about a couple of things. Is there somewhere where we could speak in private?" The sheriff asked. "Yep. Let's go back to my office." Jim replied. "Jamie, if anyone calls for me, take a message." He instructed the cashier as he led the sheriff and his deputy down the hall to his office. Jim walked into his office and motioned for the sheriff and the deputy to sit in the chairs opposite his one at his desk. "What's up, sheriff? I know you didn't stop by to shoot the bull." Jim said, still skeptical about what the sheriff wanted. "Well, Jim, I got some bad news for you. Do you know the name of the man that Lefty shot?" the sheriff asked Jim. "You mean the man who was fixing to shoot Lefty dead if he didn't defend himself?" Jim shot back. "I apologize, Jim. Yes, that man that tried to kill Lefty. Well, as you may know, the deceased gentleman's name was James Wilkins. His brother, who was arrested by the police, was named Robert Wilkins. Now, Robert Wilkins is still in jail and probably won't be getting out before we're all drawing social security, but those boys have a shit ton of cousins from down around the south where ya'll were camping. The sheriff down there called me and told me that a bunch of them have been saying they are going to make sure you, Travis, and especially Lefty gets what's coming. That's why I came here personally to give you a heads up. I know Lefty doesn't think too highly of law enforcement at this time, so I thought it would be better if I told you, and maybe you could let Lefty know what I have heard." The sheriff stopped to let his words sink in and to gauge Jim's reaction. Jim leaned back in his chair. In the back of his mind, he halfway expected this. Every Tom, Dick, and Jim Bob that those two thieving bastards are related to coming around to cause trouble was Jim's worst nightmare. Jim thought about his reply for a full minute before he spoke. "So, to be clear, you are telling me that the cousins of those two thieves, and most likely soon-to-be murderers if Lefty hadn't stopped them, are saying they are going to come up here and go after us?" Jim looked the sheriff dead in the eye. "I'm afraid so, Jim." The sheriff said. Jim cut him off from speaking further. "Sheriff, Travis, Lefty, and I have the right to defend ourselves, correct?" Jim asked. "Yes, most definitely." The sheriff answered. "OK, well, we are not going to let them shoot us, that's for goddamn sure, but we will avoid any conflict if at all possible." Jim continued. "Lefty has a hearing the day after tomorrow. If it goes well, I suspect it will piss them off more. Maybe the three of us should go stay somewhere over the weekend. Maybe enough of them have a job to have to clear out of here by next Monday." Jim stood up as he finished his sentence. He wanted to signal to the two officers that it was time for them to go so he could warn Travis and Lefty. "I think that's a good idea, Jim. If you would check in with me before ya'll leave town, I will order extra patrols by your houses to watch for anyone snooping around." The sheriff and Jim shook hands. Jim thanked them and watched them walk out of his office. Without thinking, Jim picked up the phone and called Travis. After three rings, Travis picked up and said, "I've already heard. I heard it from Chris over at the feed store." "What do you think we ought to do, Trav?" Jim asked. "I'd say we should get the hell out of town until the hearing Wednesday." Travis replied. "That's a good idea. I'll have Mike call the D.A. and see if it is kosher with him. I don't want the D.A. accusing Lefty of trying to skip town." Jim suggested. "Do it, then text me what he says." Travis replied and then hung up.

Jim called Mike and told him the situation. Mike had Jim wait on hold while he called the D.A on the other line. When Mike came on the other line, he said the D.A. approved of them leaving town until the hearing. Mike suggested Fort Smith so that they could stay downtown, where there were other people out and about usually. Jim agreed and then hung up. He texted Travis, who in turn texted Lefty. They agreed to leave that night and come back to town the morning of the hearing. By that time, it was past eleven, so Jim went out front to look for Stella. He found her helping a cashier print a report from the register. "Need to talk to you; come back to the office," Jim said. She followed him back to his office. He closed the door behind her. She kissed him, then sat on the edge of his desk. Jim sat down in the same chair the sheriff had been sitting in earlier. Jim explained the situation to her. She was concerned. "Babe, what is going to happen?" "Nothing probably; the sheriff and the D.A. think we should get out of town for the next couple of days until the hearing." Jim replied. "I need you to watch over things here for me until Wednesday. You have full authority while I'm gone. He stood up and reached in his wallet. Here is 200 extra for doing my job until Wednesday." Stella smiled broadly as she accepted the money. "Thank you! So, I won't see you tonight?" She made a show of a sad face. "Not tonight, but I'll be back Wednesday morning. I plan on coming here before the hearing." He said. "Ok, well maybe I'll meet you here so you can see me!" She said cheerfully. "Sounds like a plan." Jim replied. Stella went back to her work, and Jim left to meet Travis and Lefty for lunch.

Travis pulled up to the Mexican restaurant to find Travis and Lefty standing at the front door discussing something. Jim parked his truck, got out, and walked toward the door. "Have ya'll got it figured out yet?" Jim asked. "Yep. Tonight, we decided to get a hotel in Fort Smith, go eat somewhere nice, and get to bed early. The question is, what the hell are we going to do all day Tuesday?" Travis quizzed. "Lay low. I guess we will order room service, play cards, or something. With our luck we will get arrested for something stupid." Jim replied. "I like Jim's idea. I'm not taking any chances with this hearing hanging over my head." Lefty agreed. "Since we're all agreed. Let's eat." Travis announced as he held the door open for Jim and Lefty. They were directed toward a corner table. Lefty took the gunfighter's seat. They ordered and sat eating chips and dip while waiting for their food. "Well, Left. We could be clear of this thing Wednesday." Jim said as he reached for a chip. "God willing. It will be like a million pounds off my shoulders. Even though Mike said we have a good chance, it still feels like it's hovering over me like a guillotine ready to drop." Lefty explained. Jim was worried for Lefty. Travis's face made it clear that he was probably more worried than all of them. "We will be fine if Travis doesn't strike out on us," Lefty said, trying to hold back a laugh. "You all kiss my ass. Here I am worried about my good friend, and ya'll make fun of me." Travis shot back as he took a bite of a chip. Lefty noticed that Travis had gotten a large amount of salsa in his mustache. He jumped at the opportunity. "Trav, you got some salsa on your cheek." Lefty said. Travis grabbed his napkin and wiped his cheek. He then looked at Lefty with a totally innocent, trusting look and asked, "Did I get it?" "Yeap, you got it." Lefty answered. After their food arrived, and Travis began to eat, more and more food began to accumulate in the salsa that was stuck in Travis's mustache. Neither Jim nor Lefty informed Travis of the impending embarrassment. Finally, Travis announced that he had to piss and left the table. Lefty and Jim couldn't contain their laughter anymore. They both laughed quietly as Travis entered the bathroom. Finally, a loud "God Damnit!" could be heard from the bathroom. Travis emerged from the bathroom as Jim and Lefty erupted in laughter. "Fuck both of you. Fuck both of you straight to hell." Travis said without even a hint of a smile. "That's why the goddamn waitress kept laughing at me, wasn't it?" Travis said as he shook his head. The waitress came over to bring the check when they finished eating, and as Travis said to her, "Thank you for your hospitality, ma'am. Now, would you be so kind as to tell my companions they can pay for their own damn lunch?" They all paid out and left the restaurant. Jim and Lefty were in brighter moods than Travis.

When two o'clock rolled around, it found Lefty back at his house, preparing for a shift at his security job at the casino. He thought that he was lucky to keep his job through all of his legal jeopardy. But, in these times, natives were sticking together and standing up for each other, more so than in years past. A small few of the local white population were very vocal in their displeasure at the Supreme Court's McGirt decision, which had resulted in the Choctaw Nation's reservation being legally declared still in existence. In most cases, the vocal minority was greeted with return shouts directed back at them. The vocal minority was obviously not used to being disagreed with. Lefty never let any of the local political arguments bother him. When some half-drunk person tried to provoke him into a fight, Lefty always diffused the situation by throwing them out of the casino or bluntly telling the person that he would be banned if he didn't straighten up. None of those types of things go to Lefty, but the charges leveled against him by the D.A did get to him. It dug at his insides and his peace of mind every single minute of every single day. The whispers about him on the casino floor about his troubles were not lost on Lefty. He simply ignored them with a smile on his face, always being friendly. But on the inside, the warrior spirit of his Numunu ancestors was ready to fight back. Once he got to the casino, he focused all of his attention on his work. He clocked in, checked with the manager to see if there were any issues that needed his attention, and then he went to his post, leaving his post by the door intermittently to pace the floor and give things a look over. Most days were uneventful; this, as it would turn out, was not one of those days.

Lefty heard a bang. It sounded like someone slapping the side of a slot machine. Lefty located where the noise came from and began to slowly walk to the machine. A dark-haired lady was playing. Lefty could hear her cussing under her breath. As he approached the machine, the lady pressed the cash-out button and reached for the cash-out slip. "Everything ok, ma'am?" Lefty asked. The lady turned around, and the sight of her face sent volts of panic down Lefty's spine. "Well, hello, Lefty!" Christine, Jim's ex-wife, said. "You didn't steal my battery again, did you? Will I have to walk back home to Tulsa?" She asked, laying the sarcasm on so thick that everyone in the vicinity could pick up the vibe. "I heard you slap the machine; it is my job to make sure everything is ok." He answered, making an effort to be polite. "I'm fine. I'm going to cash out, get some gas, then head back home to Tulsa." She answered. "Good seeing you, Lefty. Take care and try to stay out of prison!" She smarted off, then walked to the cashier window. Lefty immediately found his co-worker, Jake, who was a janitor. He knew that Jake's father had dated Christine before Jim did. "Jake, do me a favor, will you go up and see if you can find out what Christine Blakely is doing in town? Here's ten dollars for your trouble." Lefty asked him to hand him a ten-dollar bill. "Hey, hell yeah. You got it!" He replied as he grabbed the money and walked off toward the cashier window. Lefty watched as Jake walked up beside Christine and feigned surprise as he patted her on the shoulder and made small talk. After a short conversation, Lefty observed Jake walk toward the bathrooms. Lefty did the same. Jake was sitting on the counter beside the sink sucking on his vape pen when Lefty walked into the bathroom. Jake started giving Lefty the information as soon as he saw him. "She says she had to come down and take care of some old insurance business on her dad's stuff. She said she's heading back to Tulsa tonight. Damn, that woman hasn't lost anything in the fine-ass department." Jake explained as he put his vape pen away. "Thanks, Jake," Lefty said. "Anytime, bro. I got to get back to work." Jake replied as he left the bathroom to get back to his rounds.

CHAPTER 16

"She's in town? You're shitting me!" Jim replied as he leaned back into his office chair. Lefty nodded his head slowly to confirm the news for Jim. "I know that bitch is crazy, and with my hearing coming up, I didn't want to call you because I know that my phones could be tapped by the D.A.," Lefty explained. "That's smart, Left. Thank you for giving me a heads up." Jim answered. "We're leaving tonight. I ain't got anything to do." Lefty asked. "Yep. Travis texted me about 20 minutes ago saying he is ready to go." Jim said. "Ok, I'm going to go pack, and then Trav and I will meet you at your house," Lefty said. "Sounds good. See you then." Jim answered. Lefty waved as he left Jim's office and headed down the hall. The rpms of Jim's mind were setting new records now. He knew from his prior encounters with Don Willis a few weeks ago that her father's estate was all settled. Jim had declined the inheritance that Christine's dad had left him due to his not updating his will after his divorce from Christine. No good was the phrase that he kept coming up with in his mind. Christine had to be up to no good, or there was some damn insurance refund she had to come sign paperwork to claim. The prior was what Jim concluded.

The Tuesday evening before the hearing, Travis, Lefty, and Jim were playing cards in the Holiday Inn in Fort Smith. They had eaten out on Monday night and Tuesday night, with both evenings turning out to be peaceful and somewhat relaxing. It felt like a break from the world, Jim thought, temporary as it was. Jim's phone rang. It was a call from his store back in Bellville. "Hello," Jim answered as he tried to stay calm until he knew what was wrong. "Jim, it is Rashad. We have a problem. The manager didn't show up today. We are really busy. Jamie is sick, so I am here by myself. I thought about calling Jack from over in Helens and see if he could come help." Rashad stopped talking as Jim cut him off. "Rash, it's ok. Jack is gone on a trip for a couple of days. I will come help you. I need something to get my mind off the hearing tomorrow anyway. I'll be there in about an hour and a half." Jim answered calmly. "Ok, boss, I am so sorry to disturb you," Rashad said in a scared, but slightly relieved voice. "It's ok. You did the right thing." Jim said, then hung up.

"What was that about?" Travis asked. "Rashad said that the manager didn't show up today, Jamie is sick, and he is there by himself. He needs help." He replied as he started to put his shoes on. "Manager? Wasn't Stella supposed to be the manager at your store until you got back?" Lefty asked as Travis picked up on what Lefty was thinking. Lefty and Travis locked eyes as they both knew that a big, loud signal from the universe was telling all three of them that trouble had occurred in paradise. "Yep, she was supposed to manage the place while I was gone. I don't know what happened, but I'm going to find out." Jim said as he stood and grabbed his cell phone and keys. "Will ya'll be ok here while I go check things out? I'm going to come back here tonight; I still don't think I should stay in Bellville until the sheriff gives us the all clear." Jim asked. "Yeah, we will be fine. I'm going to hit the sack and try to sleep while you're gone." Travis said as he stood and stretched. "Me too, I'm getting tired." Lefty agreed. Jim said goodbye and rushed to his truck.

CHAPTER 17

When Jim pulled up to his store, he saw that the parking lot was almost full, and there was a vehicle at every gas pump. "Damn," he thought. It was not normal to have this many people at his store on a Tuesday night. He parked his truck, got out, and walked to the front door. He saw Rashad at the register with a long line of customers waiting. When he noticed Jim walk behind the counter and sign into the other cash register, Rashad said, "Thank God you're here. It's been a cluster since before I called you. I don't know why all these people came in on a Tuesday."

"It's all good; we will handle it." Jim replied. They checked out customers for a solid twenty minutes before the rush subsided. Rashad went off to empty the trash cans outside that had overfilled in the absence of any help, while Jim went to his office to log in the inventory that had come in that day. He noticed an envelope taped to his computer monitor. It had "Jim" written on it in a neat cursive hand. Jim knew that it was highly likely that a woman had written it. "Great, someone is quitting at the worst possible time." He said to himself out loud. He opened the envelope and began to read.

Dear Jim,

I know this isn't a good time for you, but this would not be easy for you, no matter the circumstance. I'm sorry for not showing up today, and I'm sorry it caused problems with your plans. While I'm writing this, I think Rashad can handle the place, though that might not be the case, but you will be able to handle it regardless. I accepted a position at Bed Bath & Beyond in Fort Smith a couple of weeks ago. I also got a really nice apartment there. I didn't tell you because I wanted to make our last days together special, something we would both remember. Even though this is goodbye, this doesn't mean I don't care for you. I almost stayed. When we had that cookout at your house with Trav and Lefty, and we were all talking about how Jim finally had a girlfriend, I almost decided to stay. But the universe moves us as God wills. I'll be busy making a new life and a fresh start in Fort Smith. I hope you understand. The last time I saw you, you had a smile on your face, and that is how I will always remember you.

With all my love and best wishes,

Stella."

Jim's mind went blank. He leaned back in his chair, fighting a few tears that began to fill his eyes. He composed himself and set his brain to think. Why had she done this? Why didn't she tell him about her new job? Did she just want him for sex? All those were questions running through Jim's mind. He finally came to the conclusion that he always came to when a relationship of his ended or failed to start, which was, "The hell with it. I have work to do." After making that declaration out loud, Jim pushed the heartache out of his mind and set himself to work on the inventory.

The next morning, Travis, Lefty, and Jim found themselves eating breakfast at the café before Lefty's hearing. Lefty was taking everything better than Travis and Jim, who were visibly nervous and were unable to pour their own coffee without spilling it. Lefty had told them to let the calm, more mature Indian get their coffee ready. "So Left, what the hell actually happens this morning when we all go up to the courthouse?" Travis asked as he reached for the salt and pepper shaker. "Mike said that he will make my case to the judge by showing that the D.A. has about as much brains as Colonel Fetterman did, and then the judge will rule on whether or not the charges will be dismissed," Lefty explained. "I see, so there is a chance that this could be over today?" Travis added to his inquiry. Jim looked up at Lefty, allowing his interest in the answer to override his hunger. "According to Mike, yes." Lefty said as he scooped up some hash browns with his fork. "Damn, I hope so." Jim uttered in a soft, tired voice. "You pale faces are not as strong a people as the Numunu. They didn't call us the lords of the plains for nothing." Lefty shot back. "Very true, bub, very true." Travis agreed. They finished their breakfast in silence as each minute brought increasing amounts of nerves and worry for Travis and Jim. If Lefty was worried, he damn sure didn't show it. He was the one who grabbed the check, paid, and motivated the other two to get up off their asses and go. Lefty didn't show any worry or stress on his face, but deep down, he was a ball of nerves mixed with rage. He was angry that he was being put through this for defending the lives of himself and his friends. Now there was a chance he would be subjected to a lengthy trial and possible prison. The best-case scenario, even if the charges were dismissed, was that his reputation would be forever tarnished and his life forever changed. He knew his ancestors were a strong people. Now he asked himself if he was as strong as they were. He thought about his personal hero, the great Chief Quanah Parker. He asked himself if he could muster the same strength that Quanah Parker had shown his entire life. Lefty was determined to show dignity and strength no matter what the outcome.

The trio arrived at the courthouse 15 minutes later and met Mike Prescott just inside the front door. They all shook hands, and Mike was optimistic and upbeat. "I think we got a good chance today, boys. I really do." Mike told them. "I hope you're right, because it's about to give me and Travis a fucking stroke. "I don't see how Lefty stays so calm in times like this," Jim said to Mike. "Lefty is Numunu. His people are some of the strongest people that have ever existed." Mike shot back his short history lesson in lieu of a traditional response. "See, I told you." Lefty said. "He's got us on that one, Jim. Let's go sit down." Travis chimed in. They all shook hands as Travis and Jim went to find a seat in the courtroom. Mike and Lefty followed shortly after and sat at their table in front of the judge's throne. The nerves for Jim had started to subside by that point. Something about knowing that competent jurists were handling the problem helped soothe his nerves. He looked over at Travis. Travis was leaning back in his chair with his cap pushed back on his head, with no facial expression, which usually meant Travis was paying close attention and trying to figure out what was going on. The judge entered the room, and the bailiff hollered out. "All rise." The judge waved his hand and told everyone to sit down. Jim's heart began to pound. The moment was at hand. This could all be over in a matter of minutes, or a long ordeal could be commenced, depending on how the judge ruled. "We are here for the hearing on the defense's motion to dismiss based upon lack of evidence. Mr. Prescott, let's hear your pitch." The judge said as he opened a file folder and put on his glasses. "Thank you, your honor. We are requesting that the motion to dismiss the charges be granted due to the fact that there is absolutely no evidence that Mr. Whitehorse committed any crime in relation to the incident in question. The choice was clear; Mr. Wilkins was raising his gun to fire. Mr. Wilkins had already beaten Jim Blakely half to death. Mr. Whitehorse had a choice. Defend his and his companion's lives or face a direct short-range shot at him at the hands of Mr. Wilkins. The prosecution is pursuing these charges based solely on public pressure regarding the lenient prosecutions of unrelated cases by the District Attorney. There is no evidence that Mr. Whitehorse committed any crime. The prosecution's only witness is the cousin of Mr. Wilkins, who was committing armed robbery with Mr. Wilkins. We request that the charges be dropped, your honor. The law says Mr. Whitehorse should not be charged." Mike concluded his statement and sat down. "Ok, prosecution, down. Do you have sufficient evidence? If so, let's hear it." The assistant D.A. grabbed a yellow legal pad as he stood up and addressed the judge. "Your honor, this case does warrant these charges. The defendant does not even dispute that he shot and killed Mr. Wilkins. He shot Mr. Wilkins in cold blood, witnessed by the cousin of Mr. Wilkins. A citizen has no right to go around and doling out justice as he or she sees fit. It shows what a reckless person Mr. Whitehorse is because he did not call the police." The prosecutor stopped as the judge held up a hand. "Is it the position of the District Attorney that citizens of my district should call the police when someone is about to shoot them and not defend themselves?" The judge asked as he removed his glasses and peered down at the prosecutor. "No, your honor, it is not. Mr. Whitehorse has offered no proof that Mr. Wilkins was there to shoot or rob him, and further, Mr. Whitehorse openly admits to shooting and killing Mr. Wilkins. For all these reasons, the charges should not be dismissed. Thank you, your honor." The prosecutor quickly walked back to his table and sat down. Mike rose to speak, but the judge raised his hand and said, "That won't be necessary, counselor." The judge closed the file folder in front of him and said, "The facts in this case are easily obtained. Any reasonable person would have acted in the same manner as Mr. Whitehorse. Taking a person's life is hard on an honest man. Mr. Prescott informed me that Mr. Whitehorse has suffered great mental anxiety, worry, and pain over having taken Mr. Wilkins' life. My own wife has heard Mr. Whitehorse express in public that he wishes every day that Mr. Wilkins had not raised that gun to shoot him. The prosecution has no evidence, and furthermore, the prosecution has undertaken no effort to investigate or ascertain the reason Mr. Whitehorse defended himself. They did not interview the victims of the incident, only one of the persons who attempted armed robbery on Mr. Whitehorse and his companions. The defense's motion to dismiss the charges is granted, and the court would like to apologize to Mr. Whitehorse for the inconvenience." The judge said that, then rapped his gavel, stood, and exited the courtroom. "Now that's just, just, downright good!" Travis said, sounding at a loss for words. Jim stood up and walked over towards Lefty. Lefty had a smile on his face and was shaking hands with Mike. Lefty glanced over to Jim and met him with a hug. "Thank you, Jim. We made it. Thank you!" Lefty whispered into Jim's ear. Travis was all grins and joined in the hug shortly after. Mike shook all their hands and informed them he was off to another court hearing and said he would be in touch. After watching Mike walk out of the courtroom, Travis, Lefty, and Jim looked at each other as if they didn't know what to do. "Well, let's get some ribeyes and celebrate at Jim's house!" Lefty declared. All agreed and walked out of the courtroom to what had turned out to be the first good day in a long time.

CHAPTER 18

The light of a sunny day could be seen through the front doors of the courthouse. Travis, Jim and Lefty were all smiles. The remnants of the enormous burden that had been borne were fading away and left only the capacity for smiles and joy. The day's ruling had drowned out the dark demons of bad days of mortal existence and left optimism, appreciation for close friends, and excitement to have a day at hand. The warmth that they could feel made the day feel even better. They all walked toward Jim's truck that was parked on the side of the road in front of the courthouse. A few people walked up and down the sidewalk, but not in the amount that would constitute a crowd. Jim looked over at Lefty with a big smile on his face and placed his hand on Lefty's shoulder. "So glad to get this behind us and get out of that mess." Jim said. "Me to brother, good to feel happy again. Finally feel like I'm not a bad person. I feel good brother, I feel good." Lefty replied as they strode across the courthouse lawn toward the truck. The sound of a loud pop rang out. Jim immediately looked out into the street because it sounded like a car backfiring. He didn't see any cars anywhere close. He heard a soft thump sound and looked back toward the courthouse. He saw Travis kneel down toward the ground. Then Jim noticed blood on his left shirt sleeve. He looked over to where Lefty had been walking beside him. Lefty was lying there with a large portion of his head missing. There was a large bullet hole in the back of Lefty's head. Lefty had fallen face down on the ground. Jim immediately looked around for police, but there were already two officers running their way from the side of the courthouse. The few people that were on the courthouse lawn were looking toward the side of the courthouse where the two policemen had run from. There were three deputy sheriffs holding someone down. Jim heard one of the officers scream on the radio. "Shots fired on courthouse lawn, need ambulance immediately. I mean now!" The officers pushed Travis out of the way. Jim fell back on his butt and began to cry. Travis was weeping and cursing. Jim was paralyzed with fear. Travis suddenly jerked his head back toward the courthouse and saw the deputy sheriffs on top of a man and putting the man in handcuffs. Travis rose. Travis strode quickly toward them. Jim couldn't make himself move. He knew that three of the deputies could keep Travis under control. He looked back at Lefty. Everything had happened in what seemed like a blink of an eye. Like a slide show changing slides from a bright and beautiful day to a horror scene with a click of the controller. One of the officers tending to Lefty looked up at Jim and said, "Jim, I'm sorry, man, but he's gone. He had to be gone instantly." Jim mustered a few words through his tears. "Thank you, what do I do, who do we call?" The officer placed a hand on Jim's shoulder. "We will take it from hear. We will inform Mr. Prescott for you. Do you have anyone to call?" The cop asked. "Um, yeah, I do." Jim answered. Jim took out his phone and called his brother Eli. "Hello?" Eli said. "Brother, I need you." Jim said as he continued to fight tears. "Come to my house as soon as you can." Jim told him. Eli hadn't talked to Jim in over a month, but his only reply was simply, "On my way." As true brothers do.

The next hour was a blur. Jim didn't know what was going on and what he needed to do. He did manage to get up off of the ground and sit on a bench during that hour. Travis kept updating him every few minutes about what they were doing about Lefty's body, who the shooter was, etc. Jim heard his words, but they didn't register in his brain. Jim was even more shocked that Travis was able to function. Lefty was his best friend and a lot closer to Travis than he was to Jim. Jim slowly spoke the words to Travis. "Travis, how are you able to function? They killed him!"

Travis rubbed his eyes in an attempt to stave off an emotional meltdown. "Well, bub, I have to keep functioning and doing something. If I sit still or give myself time to think, I'll become a useless mess right here in front of people. I'm sure that will happen; I just want to be home alone when it does." He replied as he pulled his hat back down from the back of his head. "Jim, they got the shooter. Lefty is with the medical examiner. Let's go. Do you want to go to my house and get our bearings?" Travis asked as he helped Jim up off the bench. "Yes, yes, I want to go to your house. It still stings a little to smell her perfume at my house. I don't want double the emotional gut punch today." Jim responded as he gathered himself to walk to the truck. The sting and unsettling feeling that was brought on by Stella's abrupt and unexpected departure from his life was still in full swing inside of Jim. That added on to what just happened in broad daylight to Lefty, Left Jim feeling like the edge was creeping closer. The kind of creeping that occurred during the darkest times, the kind of slow creep that you never noticed until you were at the very precipice itself. Jim knew he would eventually get over Stella, but seeing Lefty facedown with a bullet hole in his head, Jim knew, would be etched in his brain forever.

After a silent 15-minute drive, they arrived at Travis's house. They got out of the truck and entered the house in silence. "Beer. Just let's sit and have a beer." Jim said. Travis made no reply; instead, he walked into the kitchen and returned with two beers. Jim sat on the couch, and Travis sat in the recliner. Finally still and in a quiet atmosphere, sleep soon overtook them both.

One hundred and twenty miles to the north, in the City of Tulsa, Christine sat on her loveseat, sipped wine, and was watching the 6:00 news. As one of the anchors was talking about the weather forecast, the screen abruptly went back to the main anchor. "Sorry Chad, we are going to have to momentarily interrupt you to bring you breaking, urgent news. In southeastern Oklahoma, in the City of Bellville, Edward Whitehorse was shot and killed on the courthouse lawn. Mr. Whitehorse had just had 2nd-degree murder charges against him dropped by a judge and was walking to his vehicle. We will update you as we receive more information on this story. Back to you, Chad." The anchor concluded. A jolt of ice-cold terror shot through Christine's body. She was completely still. The terror that was consuming her kept her frozen in place. She wondered what could have gone wrong. Surely whoever was supposed to pull the trigger knew the difference between a full-blood Comanche and a fucking white man, she told herself. She didn't know what to do. She was able to force herself to walk to her bedroom and retrieve her burner phone from the drawer of her nightstand. She dialed the number for the man she met at the Circle Cinema. It rang twice. "I know what the fuck you're going to say. I don't know what went wrong yet, but I will fucking find out. I'll call you back; don't call me." The man said and then hung up. Those words confirmed her fears; the hitman had shot Lefty by mistake. She was horrified. At that moment Christine realized something, the shock and horror that she felt now made her realize that this would not be a guilt free windfall she thought it was. She thought she hated Jim enough to go through this with no emotional scars. But now, the sorrow and terror she felt learning of Lefty's murder made her realize that she made a huge mistake. Now the big thing she had to figure out was what to do now.

That night at half past eight o'clock in the evening, Jim and Travis had concluded giving statements to the sheriff and his Napoleon of a deputy. Jim had conceded to giving his statement to Napoleon while Travis gave his statement to the sheriff. Travis had adamantly refused to speak to Napoleon, calling the deputy a "stuck-up little no-police-work-doing son of a bitch." Surprisingly to Jim, giving the statement was not as hard as he had expected. Somehow, speaking everything out loud was a kind of unexpected therapy. Despite Travis's disdain for the man, Deputy Napoleon was very professional and patient with Jim. Jim could tell he had done this type of thing before. The tears didn't hit Jim until after he had concluded his statement. It felt as if Lefty had died all over again, and the creator had hit the restart button on the grief process. Jim had given his statement on the front porch while Jim had sat at the kitchen table to give his statement. "God damn those two cops. God damn them! Making us relive that, that pure evil. Just making me say it over and over!" Travis lamented as his tears began to flow also. Travis dropped to his knees. Jim looked at Travis. The sight of Travis in the middle of the floor, sobbing, was too much for Jim to bear. The universe decided to send Eli to the rescue at the perfect time.

CHAPTER 19

Silence had ruled ever since Eli had entered Travis's house, got Travis off the floor, and calmed Jim down to where he could control himself. Eli had told Jim and Travis that he had stopped at the sheriff's office to find out where Jim was after Eli had first gone to Jim's house. The trio had migrated to the back porch and had begun to drink a few beers to calm everyone's nerves. "Ok guys, you think you can tell me what you know about what happened without getting too upset?" Eli asked. "Well, I have to start talking at some point. It is against my nature to be this quiet for this long. So, I'll go first. We were walking to the truck across the courthouse lawn, and someone fired a shot and hit Lefty in the head. We didn't see the shooter; we both heard the shot, and the next thing we knew, we saw Lefty on the ground. At least he didn't suffer, or at least that's what one of the cops told me." Travis explained. "I'm wondering who the fuck did it!" Jim added. "The sheriff said he will give us an update when he knows more," Travis replied. "Good, it's burning up my insides not knowing who did this," Jim said as he got up to get another round of beers. When Jim returned with the beers, Eli accepted one as Jim held one out for him and said, "Jim, seeing that I used to work in your store a few years back, and I know your system, how about I go handle your store for you tomorrow so you can rest up? Do you want me to give you a ride home?" Eli said as he looked at Jim, waiting for his answer. Travis chimed in, "Jim continued his shitty streak with women yesterday evening. The girl he was fucking left him a Dear John letter at his office. She did that after she took his two hundred extra dollars for managing the store for him. Took his money and got the hell out of dodge. Jim, that's why you don't pay hookers or preachers up front. That way they have to fuck you with you watching." This got Eli's attention and brought a big smile. "Atta boy, Jim!" Eli said. "Hell, I'm just glad you actually took some interest in a female other than Christine!" He congratulated Jim and took a drink of his beer. "For the record, damnit, I am not heartbroken; I'm royally pissed off. The bitch left me high and dry at the store, and she knew Rashad would be there alone, and she skipped town anyway. The least she could have done was wait at least one fucking day!" Jim complained. This type of conversation was Travis's forte, and Travis knew it, so he jumped at the opportunity to share his wisdom. "Hell, that's just this younger generation now. They don't know what the hell loyalty is. They don't know what the hell common courtesy is, and they damn sure don't have the same kind of work ethic as we do! She left at a bad time because she was concerned about herself and no one else!" Travis roared as he stood to drive home his conviction. "Sounds like it's a good thing you found out what kind of person she was when you did; it could have wound up being worse down the road." Eli concurred as Travis raised his beer bottle to signal that he was appreciative that Eli agreed with him. Jim raised his glass to join the informal toast and said, "On to the next woman!" Jim leaned back in his chair, looked at Eli, and said, "I'll be torn up for a while over Lefty, but I think the sheer pain of losing a best friend has pretty much made the pain of losing a girlfriend seem insignificant. So, I think I'll be ok to go back home." As they started to leave, Jim and Travis decided to try to stay in close proximity to each other in the next few days so that either one of them could rescue the other if they had another breakdown. As soon as Jim got to his bed, he was fast asleep.

At seven am, the daily luminescent being was making its way through Jim's bedroom window. The sunshine looked like a futuristic portal waiting to transport Jim away from this world into another dimension of mortal bliss. Jim rose to his feet through the daydreams and temptations to sleep all day and made his way to his bathroom for a refreshing shower. After dressing and emerging from the bedroom and into the living room, he found Eli sitting on the couch putting on his shoes. "Morning, bro. How you feeling?" he asked. "As well as could be expected I guess." Jim answered. "I'm going to head to your store and make sure things are squared away and keep the place from burning down. Anything special going on?" Eli asked as he grabbed his keys and headed for the front door. "Nothing special, just normal. Shouldn't be too busy. I know I need to rest, but I think I will head down to the store and relieve you after lunch. I just feel the need to get out and keep a somewhat normal schedule." Jim said as he sat down in the recliner. "Might do you good. But take some time and rest up this morning. Call me if you need me before then." Eli said as he waved goodbye and headed out the door.

A few minutes later, Jim's phone beeped. He had a text message from Travis. It read "Meet me at the café in 20 minutes. Important. Can't tell you on the phone." Jim thought for a minute after he read the message. He typed out a reply that read. "Can't handle anymore tragedy today. If its horrible news I'm staying home." "It's not tragic, just suspicious." Was Travis's answer. Jim finally let curiosity get the better of him and made his way to the café.

Jim walked into the café half an hour later and looked around the place for Jim. He saw her sitting at a table on the side of the room, taking a drink of coffee. Jim walked over and sat down. "So, what did you do, where did it happen, and how many people are after you?" Jim mocked as he sat down. Travis looked up from his coffee with a look of extreme concern on his face. "The bitch is here." He said. "Who's here? Jim asked. "Your bitch of an ex-wife is in town," Travis said. Cold shots of sheer dread shot down Jim's spine. He tried hard not to let his face contort into a ball of rage when he heard the words come out of Travis's wife. Jim didn't say anything in response. The look on Jim's face gave Travis all the information he needed to know how Jim felt about the news. "I can't get the thought out of my head, Jim. Lefty winds up shot, and the next thing we know, the bitch is in town." Travis said as he shook his head. "That just seems like it may be a tad bit stronger than a coincidence." "Yes, it is." Jim said. "Fuck, I won't sleep at night now" Jim lamented as he relaxed and leaned his head back and stared up at the ceiling. Jim's and Travis's phone beeped almost simultaneously. Jim reached and grabbed his phone and read the message. It was from Eli, and the message read. "You need to get down to the store now. Pretty sure your ex-wife just walked in the door." Jim looked up from his phone toward Travis. Without even knowing what the message said, Travis shot Jim a knowing glance. They paid for their food and left.

Jim had a million thoughts running through his head. The first thing he had done was install a voice recording app on his phone. There was no way that Jim was ever going to let himself be put in a situation where it was this lying bitch's word against his. He felt nervous but also prepared. Fifteen minutes later he pulled up to his store and sat for a moment to see what all was going on. There weren't many people there at that moment, and he couldn't see Christine anywhere. He worked up his nerve and got out of his truck. As he began walking toward the front door, he spotted Christine as she walked up to the cashier and placed a drink on the counter. Seeing someone significant from the past, or in Jim's case, seeing an ex-wife, gives one a glimpse into a life left behind. It was like a slow-motion slideshow of what might have been, had it not been for a few good decisions or bad decisions, however you wanted to look at it. Jim forced the old emotions back down and opened the front door and walked in. When the door dinger went off to signal that someone had just entered the front door, Christine turned and looked toward the front door. Jim saw that look. It was the same look she had given him a million times before. It was the same way she looked at him after she almost burned down the house when she was trying to cook their first meal together. Jim also saw that look on her face shortly before she had confessed to having an affair with Jim's boss. When Christine turned to look at Jim when he walked in the door, Jim knew instantly that Christine had fucked up somehow.

CHAPTER 20

"Hello Christine, what brings you here to ruin my day?" Jim said bluntly. "Can we go somewhere and talk?" she said. "In my office," Jim said as he walked past her. She followed him down the hall into his office. Jim closed the door to the office behind them. Christine sat down in a chair in front of Jim's desk, and Jim sat down heavily into his chair behind his desk. "OK, what's going on?" Jim asked without showing any expression on his face. She wiped a tear from her eye and let out a deep breath. "Jim, what I'm about to tell you will send me to prison. But I can't let anything else happen. I have to tell you." She said, fighting back tears. "What the fuck did you do?" Jim asked as he stood. "Jim, I took out a life insurance policy on you while we were married. I paid the premiums from my own account. Jim, I was broke and didn't know what to do. I met a man who told me about a person who took care of problems." She stopped talking as Jim cut her off. "You mean you fucked some random stranger from some cocktail bar who blabbed everything he ever knew about anything." Jim said as he continued to stare at Christine blankly. "Basically yes," Christine admitted. "I spoke with a man, and I paid him ten thousand dollars to kill you. When I heard about Lefty on the news, I couldn't bear the guilt I felt. Lefty was totally innocent, and he died because of me. "Because of my greed, Lefty is dead." Christine was fighting to get her words out through tears at this point. Jim was shocked at this news, but surprisingly, he was not surprised. He retrieved his phone from the front pocket of his shirt and pretended like he was checking his phone for messages. He saw that the phone was still recording. Jim was getting her confession on tape, just as he had hoped. Now she could never lie about how this conversation went. Jim had also called Eli on his way over and instructed him on how to turn on the security camera in his office, which also happened to record audio as well. Jim thought long and hard about what to do next.

"Ok, tell me everything. Who did you contact and tell me everything that was said?" Jim ordered. Christine sighed, gathered herself, and began. She told Jim everything. She told him about the first meeting with the man at the Circle Cinema and the phone conversation she had with the man after she heard about Lefty. Jim stood up again and turned and looked out the window behind his desk. Christine was still crying. Jim knew that he had her. He had the information that would send her to prison. He thought for a few minutes longer before saying anything. Then he turned and looked straight at her. "Do you know who shot Lefty?" Jim asked her. "When I met the man at the circle cinema, he told me he was planning on getting someone named Carlo Manfredi to do it." She answered. "And you think the bullet was meant for me, I take it? Because you wanted the payoff from the life insurance policy?" Jim asked. Christine told him again about the phone conversation she had with the man after she had seen the news report about Lefty. Jim knew that if this Carlo guy was the shooter, then he was locked up in the county jail and wouldn't see the light of day for the rest of his life most likely. "Have you talked to the man who sent Carlo anymore?" Jim asked. "No, not since the day of Lefty's shooting." She answered. "Call him or find out who he is. I don't care who you have to blow to get the information, but you better get it, or I'll send this recording to the D.A." he told her coldly. "Recording? What are you talking about?" Christine said as she stood up with a panicked looked on her face. "I'm recording this conversation. Audio and video. I'm recording this because I don't fucking trust you." Jim told her. Reality hit Christine as she knew that Jim had her dead to rights. Jim knew he had complete control over her. "Go find out who this fuck is. When you find out who it is come back here. Not my house, here." Jim ordered. Christine gathered her emotions and said, "Ok, I'll see what I can do." She stood up and looked back at Jim once before she left and headed down the hall and exited the store. Jim walked into the small closet where his computer server was and turned off the audio recording feature in his office. He walked up to the front counter and found Eli. He wasn't going to let Eli in on what he had just learned from Christine. He didn't want to drag Eli into this mess. "Hey bro, how did it go with the black widow in there?" Eli asked as he wiped down a counter with a rag. "Same old bullshit, wanting a loan and offered to do whatever I wanted to get it." Jim lied as he leaned up against the counter. "Damn, I would have at least tried to get some of that before I told her to leave." Eli joked. "That bitch is evil, her snatch probably has teeth in it now." Jim shot back. Eli finished up cleaning and Jim told him that he was ok to take over. Jim walked Eli to his vehicle, gave his brother a hug, and thanked him for helping out when Jim needed it. Eli waved to Jim as he pulled out of the parking lot. Jim took out his phone and called Travis. "Hello," Travis answered. "Meet me at your house this evening about 5:30," Jim said.

When Jim arrived back home at a few minutes after five o'clock, he grabbed a beer from his refrigerator and sat on the front porch to wait for Travis to arrive. As Jim sat in a lawn chair on his front porch, his foot tapped nervously. The rapid tapping was eerily reminiscent of some core of drummers sending out a drum roll, setting the scene for reality to reach its climax. Jim's nerves eased when he saw Travis's gray Ford truck coming up the driveway. Jim sat back in his chair. Travis parked his truck, retrieved a beer from Jim's refrigerator, and found a lawn chair beside Jim. "Well, my blood pressure has been elevated, so do you want to enlighten me?" Travis said as he opened his beer. Jim let out a deep breath and started. "When I got to the store, Christine was waiting out front by the counter. I took her into the office and recorded the whole conversation." Jim said and he took a drink of his beer. Jim told him the whole conversation that he and Christine had. When Jim told Travis that Christine had hired a hitman to kill Jim and that he had killed Lefty by mistake, Travis stood up as the shock and anger were too much to bear. "That fucking evil cunt!" he yelled. Travis's anger echoed through the trees and seemed to go on forever. As tears of rage poured down Travis's face, Jim became concerned. He had never seen Travis break under pressure before. But the intense pressure of this moment was too much for any mortal man to take without reacting as Travis had. "Her fucking greed!! She's fucking insane, Jim! What the fuck are we going to do now?" Travis asked as he looked to his friend for some kind of reassurance. "I don't..." Jim's words trailed as his phone began to ring. He saw that it was Christine. "Talk." Jim ordered as he answered the call. Christine began to speak, and he put the call on speakerphone. "Start over." Jim ordered and Christine began again. "He answered when I called him. The guy who I first met with, I mean. He is going to meet with me again." She explained. "Where?" Jim asked. "My house on Saturday evening around 11." She answered. Jim replied only, "OK." He hung up and looked up at Travis. "So, what now? Is she going to get the lowdown on this guy? Is she going to call him off?" Travis asked in rapid succession. "That's what she thinks," Jim replied. Jim then told Travis his plan.

CHAPTER 21

Friday night, 8 pm at Travis's House.

Instead of cooking, Jim had picked up supper from the local BBQ restaurant. He stopped by a local thrift store to look through books. Digging through the cheap books that only cost a couple of dollars and finding a gem helped take Jim's mind off trouble. That was the case today, more so than normal. When he concluded his purchases and with food in hand, he drove to Travis's house. Jim had been going over details in his mind ever since Thursday evening. Jim's phone rang as he was pulling up to Travis's house. Jim shut his truck off and answered it, "Hello." "We got your repair order done, sir. Left everything where you instructed. I left an invoice in the mailbox." The man on the other end of the line said. "Thank you, appreciate it," Jim said, then hung up. With the call concluded and his resolve strengthened, he got out of his truck and went inside. "Repairs get finished?" Travis asked as Jim walked into the house. "Yep, and the repair guy left everything on site, and it's all done," Jim replied as he sat down sacks of food on the dining table. "Good. I got my shit ready. "Have you come to terms with what we're doing?" Travis asked. "It was my idea, remember?" Jim shot back. "I know, just making sure you're good with everything. "Because there won't be any going back," Travis said. "A man once sang a song," Jim replied. "You can run on for a long time, but sooner or later God will cut you down." Jim sang out loud the words from the famous Johnny Cash song. Jim sat silently for a moment and let his thoughts go where they may. What could go wrong? Was this absolutely necessary to save his or both of their lives? Could they be walking into something they didn't anticipate? "Trav." Jim said as he looked out towards the far horizon. "What?" Travis replied as he looked over at his old friend. "Is this the best thing to do?" He asked as he took his eyes off of the horizon and looked down at his boots. "Jimmy, I think that if we do nothing, sooner or later some son of a bitch is going to want to clean up some loose ends. Lucky for us, we know what the hell is going on. They damn sure aren't expecting two hillbillies like us to come up to Tulsa County guns a-blazin'!" Travis confidently announced. "Yep. That's what I keep telling myself." Jim paused his words as he stood. "Let's go."

The tick of the clock rang out like a hammer pounding on a nail. The sound of each tick shot nerves and fear through Christine's body. The clock said 10:59, and the man was supposed to be there at eleven. Christine did not know what door the man would enter through. She had been instructed to leave all of her doors open and to be sitting at her dining table by eleven. She heard her back door open. Her heart started pounding. She did not want to meet with the man again, but she had no choice. Jim had all the evidence he needed to send her to prison for a very long time. She had to get Jim the information he wanted. She had no clue what Jim would do with the information, but she guessed that he only wanted to know who was after him and that he was going to try to stop them somehow. The man emerged through her back door beside her kitchen. "Hello, is anyone home?" The man's gravelly voice echoed throughout the kitchen. The man walked into the area off the kitchen where Christine's dining table was. "There you are." The man said as he sat down. "Ok, here's what happened. Carlo hired a shooter to take out your ex-beau. The guy obviously fucked up and missed the target and hit this Comanche gentleman. But rest assured, we'll get him. I'm taking over the job. Carlo, well, he has been, let's say, reassigned." The man explained. The man stood up and said, "That's all for now. I'll keep you updated." He turned to leave, then said, "I almost forgot; I do have something for you." He pulled out a silenced pistol and fired two shots into Christine's head. Then, he calmly put the pistol away and exited the way he came with a feeling of satisfaction and closure.

10 miles away Travis and Jim were northbound with pistols ready. With every mile, they got angrier. They were angry about Lefty, angry at the asshole who shot Lefty, and angry at the world in general. Travis had begun to calm down on the drive up, but it didn't change his dedication to getting revenge. They had driven in silence the entire time until Travis said, "I have to hear some music or noise or something," as he turned on the radio. Travis flipped through radio station after radio

station and finally gave up. "There isn't anything but pure shit on the radio now. No beat, no melody, just hollering and banging on boxes and a bunch of Nashville people that want to sound like rappers so bad they can't stand it." Travis lamented as he leaned back into his seat. The pair closed in on their destination and had no idea what awaited them.

The man had cleaned up a loose end well. He didn't delegate this one; he wanted to do it himself. If no one knew, then no one could talk. With his task complete, he walked through the backyard and exited the backyard through a side gate and quickly stepped into the shadow side of the house that shielded him from the light of the closest streetlamp. "What the fuck is this?" he thought to himself. There was a fuckin' cowboy and a redneck-looking guy waiting there. What idiots they were. The redneck heard him and spun around. "Freeze, you shit-kicking motherfucker!" The man yelled as he beat the redneck and the cowboy, getting the drop on them before they could raise the pistols they had in their hands. The man kept his gun trained on the cowboy and pulled a second pistol from his coat and aimed it at the redneck. This was not part of the plan.

"Jim, whatever you do, don't move. I got this one." Travis instructed. "You're awfully confident there, blonde." Jim said, shooting back the reference to the Clint Eastwood movie, "The Good, Bad and the Ugly." "Damn right." Travis slowly stepped closer to the man holding up the two guns and continued in a slow, clear voice. "Jim, I don't know which one of us is the good one and which one of us is the bad one, but I damn sure know who the ugly one is here," Travis said as he slowed his breathing. "It's this ignorant piece of...." At that moment, the gunshot roared. The man fell dead with a bullet hole where his left eye had been moments earlier. "Been practicing that one, bud." Travis said as he reached down and picked up his shell casing and said, "Let's go, no time to sit and chat." Jim followed Travis back into the shadows, across two alleyways, and finally back to the truck. "Now, Jim. Let's go home and forget this night ever happened."

www.ingramcontent.com/pod-product-compliance
Lightning Source LLC
LaVergne TN
LVHW010931110826
845149LV00013B/2542
9781971232652